PHONE CALLS

ANN REIT

SCHOLASTIC INC.
New York Toronto London Auckland Sydney Tokyo

For Grandma—who was always there

Cover Photo by Owen Brown

ISBN 0-590-32189-7

Copyright © 1983 by Ann Reit. All rights reserved. Published by Scholastic Book Services®, a division of Scholastic Inc.

12 11 10 9 8 7 6 5 4 3 2   3 4 5 6 7 8

Printed in the U. S. A.   06

PHONE CALLS

A Wildfire Book

Chapter One

As I walked home from school on a cold, gray, end-of-January afternoon, I thought that if I hadn't been named Juliet my life would have fewer problems. I had a very definite picture of what *the* Juliet — the one who went with Romeo — looked like. I knew she was small, feminine, with black hair that fell below her waist, and a luscious mouth. I also knew she had inspired passion in every man she met.

I wished I looked like that, but I didn't. I was tall and very slim, with long legs. My hair was dark blond and curly, cut close to my head, and I had hazel eyes, not brown or golden but somewhere in the

1

middle. I had not inspired passion in any man I knew, and Romeo wouldn't have given me a second look.

I pulled the collar of my down jacket closer to my neck and walked up the block. As I approached my house, I looked at it the way a stranger might. It was an old, Victorian structure, very big, and built of gray stone with what should have been sparkling white trim. The stone was weathered and worn and the trim badly needed painting. It made me think of all the things that badly needed *something*. Since my father had died six years ago, when I was ten, my mother had just managed to hang on to the house we all loved, and there hadn't been enough money to keep everything painted, repaired, and working.

As I walked into the quiet hall of the house, I called out, "Grandma, I'm home."

When I heard her answering voice say, "I'm upstairs, Juli. In my room," I felt a familiar, all's-right-with-the-world warmth. Grandma was there.

I ran up the stairs and into Grandma Lang's room. It was fixed as a sitting room. Against one wall was a large studio couch covered with a soft, emerald green velvet bedspread and piled high with pale green pillows. Matching green velvet draperies framed the windows softly, giving the room an elegant look. The bureau and desk were of dark, polished wood that almost gleamed. The fact that everything had seen better days didn't detract from the richness of the room.

Harriet Lang was my mother's mother. She was a small, compact woman with pale blue eyes and gray hair that curled around her face. She was sitting in a comfortable gold club chair, knitting a sweater for me. She lifted her eyes from her favorite soap opera, which she was watching intently, and motioned silently to me. I sat on the floor in front of her, with my back resting against her knees, took a pear from the bowl of fruit that was on a table next to her chair, and watched the set quietly until the program ended.

"What happened today?" I pointed to the TV set.

"Well," Grandma said, "Amanda has decided not to tell Gerald that she had been married before and that her first husband is now in jail, because she thinks that Cynthia will use it against her in some way."

I shook my head. "Not wise. It is all going to end in disaster."

Grandma ran her hand through my hair

3

and laughed. "Of course, it is. It has to compete with all the other daytime disasters."

I turned and touched the sweater Grandma was knitting and said wistfully, "It's so pretty. You spoil me, Grandma."

"I know I do," Grandma Lang said with satisfaction. "It's one of the pleasures of being a grandmother." She went back to her knitting. "Your mother called. She's working a little late tonight so we won't have dinner until around seven-thirty. How about some tea to tide us over?"

"Great. I'll help you make it."

We went down to the kitchen, and as I set out the cups on the table, I watched Grandma at the stove and felt an almost painful surge of love for her. She had come to live with us after my father died. She ran our house with enthusiasm and efficiency, while my mother worked as a legal secretary in a law office in the small Connecticut city where we live. In the years that Grandma had been with us, she and I had formed a bond of love and closeness that had become my delight and almost the foundation of my life.

Now Grandma turned from the stove and asked, "Cinnamon toast?"

"I'd love it, but Mother won't approve of all the sugar, sugar, sugar."

Grandma reached for the bread. "Well, I'd say that what your mother doesn't know won't hurt her . . . or us." She bent down and held a match to the gas under the broiler and waited for it to catch. "The stove needs checking, I think."

I looked around the large, comfortable kitchen. It was bright and cheerful, filled with plants, the walls painted a pale orange. A wild assortment of pots and utensils hung on the walls. But the linoleum had worn spots on it, and every electrical appliance groaned, complained, and shuddered when it was turned on. Everything worked — for now — but it seemed just a matter of time before something gave up and expired.

As Grandma and I sat at the table eating, I asked, "Where's Barbara?"

"She's studying at Alfie's house."

I put down my cup. "I can't stand it. There's Barbara, my 'baby' sister, fourteen years old, and already she has an almost-steady boyfriend. And here I am, named after Juliet yet, and look at me. Do you know, a new kid in school said the same thing to me today that thousands of other

5

kids have said? He passed me in the hall, looked at me slyly, and asked, 'Where's Romeo?' "

Grandma was about to say something, but I went right on. "Why, tell me, why did Mother have to name me Juliet? It's caused me nothing but trouble. It's a burden, a trial, and a pain in the neck."

Grandma Lang put a piece of toast in her mouth. "Are you through?"

I nodded.

She looked at me with a puzzled expression on her face. "I don't understand you. When I was growing up, if a girl had two boyfriends — count them, two — like you have, she would have thought Juliet was the perfect name for her. Look at you, you have Mike and Cliff. Mike is a lovely boy and Cliff . . . well, Cliff is a little strange, but he's nice, too, I'm sure."

I tried to explain patiently. "Grandma, they aren't boyfriends. They are just friends who happen to be boys. I don't feel anything different for them than I feel for Midge."

Grandma thought for a moment. "You go to the movies with them, to dances, to parties, don't you?"

I nodded.

Grandma nodded, too. "Then they're boyfriends, as far as I'm concerned."

I laughed. "You're the most stubborn woman I know. I go to parties and movies with Midge, too. We just all go together. It isn't a *date*."

I rinsed the cups and saucers and put them in the dishwasher. "I hope there's more in store for me than that. They're nice, Grandma, but I don't feel anything romantic for Mike or Cliff."

Grandma walked over to me and held me close. "I know what you mean, Juli. It will come. Really."

I leaned against her comforting softness and smelled the faint scent of a flowery cologne, apple blossoms. I hugged her and said, "I think I'll go up and do some homework if you don't need any help with dinner."

Grandma swatted me gently on the rear. "Go ahead. Everything is under control."

My bedroom always made me feel as if it were spring, even when the sounds of the overworked furnace denied it. When Grandma Lang had come, I had given up my large room and moved into what had been my father's den. It was small, but I loved it. The roof sloped down to a sharp low eave and under the slope was my bed. The walls of the room, and the sides and ceiling of the eave were covered with a flowered blue wallpaper, so that when I lay on my bed and looked up, I felt as if I were under an arbor. The bed had a blue spread that almost matched the wallpaper, and crisp, white organdy curtains drifted over the window that was a couple of feet from the head of the bed. A rosy rug was on the floor. The only other furniture in the room was a small chest, a desk and chair, and a bookcase that held my favorite books.

I lay down on the bed and turned my head to look out of the window at the purple, winter evening sky. I glanced at the outline of what would become a bright moon and thought about Timothy Thornton.

The only person in the world who knew I was in love with Timothy Thornton was Midge Roth, my best friend. I knew that all of history had been filled with hopeless loves, but I felt mine was the most hopeless. It would have been just too embarrassing to tell anyone else, even Grandma, that I loved a boy who was only politely aware of me.

Timothy had spoken to me that day, and I didn't know which was worse: the days he didn't speak to me at all, the days I didn't see him, or the days when we exchanged a few words.

It wasn't sensible to love Timothy Thornton, and I was a sensible girl. Everyone said so. Everyone said to my mother, "It must be so nice to have a sensible daughter like Juliet, not irresponsible like so many young people these days."

I was the kind of girl who always did her homework on time; who got up early enough to eat breakfast; and who never kept anyone waiting, not even the dentist. So to be in love with a rare boy like Timothy was not like me.

Timothy Thornton was one of the beautiful people of Dellwood High School. He looked beautiful, he acted beautiful, and his friends were the other beautiful people. He was tall and thin and had shining blond hair and greenish-brown eyes. He moved with sureness and grace. His voice was deep and low, and when he laughed he threw back his head and put his whole being into it, making the world light up.

To me he was every movie hero, every charismatic public figure, every brave knight in shining armor. He was near, but inaccessible. For me to love him was pointless and stupid — and true.

What made it harder to bear was that Timothy was a nice person. We had grown up in the same town, and whenever we were at a dance he would dance exactly one dance with me. Whenever we were at a party he would come over and say hello. And if we met in the halls at school, as we had that day, he would stop and talk to me. Sometimes I wished he would just totally ignore me. Then a sensible girl like me wouldn't even have anything to dream about.

I thought of a line from an Emily Dickinson poem: *"He put the Belt around my life/I heard the Buckle snap."* That's the way I felt about Timothy, as if he had surrounded my life in some way.

"Insane," I said to myself. Especially since Tim was unaware that his belts and buckles had anything to do with me.

"Obsessive," Midge said. And she was right.

My feelings for Timothy Thornton went so deep that one day sensible Juli had picked up a candy wrapper he had thrown away. I had carefully spread it out and smoothed away the creases. The wrapper had rested in the corner of my top drawer for a year, and every now and then I would take it out and just look at it. Then I would carefully fold it again and put it away. Even Midge didn't know *that*.

As I lay on the bed I whispered aloud. "He put the Belt around my life." I wondered why most teachers hid the fact that Emily Dickinson was such a wonderful poet, one that girls could really learn something from. They made us learn, "There is no Frigate like a Book," which always bored me, and never told us that Emily knew about belts and buckles snapping, too.

Chapter Two

The sound of a dish breaking in the kitchen woke me suddenly. I sat up and shivered. The furnace had stopped for a while, having decided the house had reached the proper temperature. My room, which an hour before had been warm and filled with winter twilight, was now cold and shadowed by the night. I reached down and pulled over me a multicolored afghan Grandma had knitted. I huddled underneath it and realized I had fallen asleep while I had been thinking about Emily Dickinson's belt.

I heard my mother saying, "Barbara, if I had a dollar for every dish you break I would be rich." Her voice was filled with irritation.

Then she called, "Juliet, where are you? Dinner is ready."

"I'll be down in a minute, Mom."

I went in the bathroom and washed my face with icy water, trying to wake up. I combed my hair and ran down the stairs. Everyone was in the dining room, and Grandma was dishing out the food. Our dining room was for more than dining, and it looked that way. Three walls were lined with bookcases and against the fourth was an old upright piano piled high with books and sheets of music. My father had loved to play old songs and had collected all the old sheet music he could find. I never looked at the piano without thinking of the nights he had dragged all of us into the dining room, insisting on singing the songs he loved.

I went over to my mother and kissed the top of her head, then I sat down in my seat at the table. She smiled at me. "Hi. You were as quiet as the proverbial mouse up there."

I smiled back and said, "I fell asleep. It's this hectic social life that's wearing me out."

She looked wistful as she answered. "I know what you mean. The constant round of parties and balls."

The look on Mother's face hurt me. My mother was beautiful, with hair the color of mine that curled the way mine did, but hers was baby fine. Her eyes were blue, like Grandma's, but they were bright, bright blue, and had a look of innocence that always startled me. Her nose was straight and classic, but it had the slightest bump in the middle where it had been broken as a child. Her skin was almost translucent and never blemished in any way. Once she had been laughing and playful, but now she was quiet, and there were faint blue smudges under her eyes. I knew she was tired most of the time — and worried.

Mother was looking at the huge platter of chicken paprika Grandma was dishing out. "Ma, you work too hard. You don't have to cook banquets like this every night. We'd all survive."

Grandma kept putting pieces of chicken floating in sour cream gravy on the plates. "Elizabeth, you're the daughter, and I'm the mother. I'm old enough to know what I want to do and what I like to do. Your job is to work and bring in some money; mine is to take care of the house. Okay?"

We all laughed, and Mother said reluctantly, "Okay." But I saw the look that passed between them. It was one of caring and admiration, and I hoped that when I was older I would exchange looks like that with my mother. For now, I cut into the chicken that was on my plate surrounded by what Grandma called *nockerle*, which were tiny dumplings. Grandma's parents had been Hungarian, and she cooked things like the chicken and nockerle from recipes her mother had given her. We all loved them and kept telling her how happy we were that she had Hungarian parents.

Barbara, who sat opposite me, put her fork down and cleared her throat. As she did, she gave me a pleading look. It was a look I knew, one that begged, *help*.

"Ma, Joy is having a party Saturday night and wants me to sleep over. I can, can't I?" Barbara tilted her head, surrounded by long, shining brown hair, to the side. Her huge brown eyes gazed at Mother innocently.

Mother ignored the studied innocence and said firmly, "No."

15

Barbara sat up straighter. "Mother, why not? You're not being fair."

Mother speared three nockerle with her fork. "Because after the party, Alfie will stay late and Joy's boyfriend will stay late, and I want you home."

Tears filled Barbara's eyes. She was the best at on-demand tears of anyone I knew. "Her parents will be there. You don't trust me. If it was Juli, you'd let her stay. Wouldn't you?"

Mother looked at me and then at Barbara. "Barb, I trust you, and yes, if it were Juli I'd let her stay. Juli is sensible."

I shook my head. "Right! Juli is sensible. Why doesn't someone ever say, 'Juli is fascinating. Juli is exotic. Juli is adorable.'"

I saw my mother's mouth tighten slightly, the way it did when she was angry or annoyed. "Don't put down sensible. You may spend part of your life or all of your life on your own, and sensible will be something that will come in handy."

Then she relaxed, and a sweet smile eased the tight line of her mouth. "Have I told you that Eve Ellison called me yesterday? The whole family is moving back here in a couple of weeks. Frank Ellison

16

has a new job, and Eve is going to open a boutique. You and Oliver were once quite close, Juli. Maybe he's what you're looking for."

I laughed in amazement. "Mom, Oliver and I were twelve when he left town. We'd hardly know each other now."

Barbara smiled in a mean way, looked straight at me, and said, "You haven't changed at all. You just got taller."

I knew she was angry at me because I hadn't jumped in and asked Mother to let her stay at Joy's. But I didn't feel like being noble at the time. Barbara's having a boyfriend, even a dummy like Alfie, made me jealous, even though I hated to admit it. I gave Barb as cool and condescending a look as I could muster. "It's so nice to have a supportive sister."

"Isn't it?" she said just as coolly.

Mother looked at us both wearily. "Can it! Be civilized for one meal. Or at least try!"

17

Chapter Three

The next morning as I walked to school I slowed up when I got to Midge's house. We were best friends, but neither one of us felt we had to be glued to each other. If we happened to meet on the way to school we enjoyed it, but we never arranged it in advance. But I was happy to see her run down the walk from her door and catch up with me. I was feeling troubled and needed her sanity.

Midge Roth was a small, rounded girl. She just hit five-one, and the two of us made a strange combination that we often giggled over. Her eyes were a sharp blue,

18

and her nose and mouth were small and pretty. Everyone thought Midge was the "sweetest" girl in Dellwood, and she was. But what most people weren't aware of was that behind that good-girl exterior were an inquiring mind and a quick sense of humor. We were very different, but there was nothing I couldn't say to Midge, or didn't. We might argue, but she was always open and loving.

We walked along in silence for a few blocks. I huddled as deep in my jacket as I could, hating the biting winter air. She walked with her coat flying open, her cheeks rosy. "Isn't the air gorgeous?" she asked, breathing deeply.

"Gorgeous," I mumbled, making a face at her.

She put her arm around my waist and gave me a small hug. "You have no blood."

I hugged her back and said, "Midge, did you know Oliver is coming back to town?"

"Don't you think I would have told you, if I'd known? When is he coming and how do you feel about it?" She paused. "It must be funny seeing a boy you haven't seen for four years."

"It doesn't feel funny or not funny," I

said. "I guess it will be nice to see him again. I used to like him. You know, as a friend-type boy."

Midge breathed deeply. "You have more friend-type boys than anyone I know. And the only boy you don't think of as a friend has to be Mr. Beautiful Person of the whole town. You sure make it hard on yourself."

I snuggled deeper into my coat and shook my head with confusion. "I know. And to change the subject, but not really, are you coming to the basketball game tonight?"

"Are you going?" Midge asked.

"Sure. Mike would feel bad if I didn't watch him play. He thinks I bring him luck. It's the biggest game of the year, so I really want to see him win."

"Don't you ever wish he'd lose, just for a change?" Midge grinned as she spoke. "Just to shake the perfect Mike O'Connell athlete image."

"Boy, for the 'sweetest girl in town,' you can certainly be surprising." I poked her in the arm and then remembered. "Oh, you don't mind if Cliff sits with us, do you?"

Midge stopped walking and leaned over to tie her sneaker. As she stood up, she sighed. "I don't mind, if he stops examining everybody's slightest thought and action. He can really be a drag."

I defended Cliff Quincy halfheartedly. "He's a very thoughtful guy. He can't help it. It's just the way he is. I think he'll probably become something very special like a psychiatrist or — who knows what."

Midge laughed. "Who knows what is right. Doesn't he ever just let himself enjoy life, without wondering *if* he's enjoying it, and if he is, *why* he is?"

That night at the game I thought about what Midge had said. Actually, I liked Cliff the way he was, and often we sat for hours analyzing life and why people did what they did. I sat between Cliff and Midge and watched Mike O'Connell being the star athlete he was, running all over the court doing everything right. I liked the way Mike was, too, and we went biking together and played tennis and hiked. I seemed to be the girl for all seasons for both of them. We were buddies. They felt about me the way I felt about them — friendly. Neither one of them had ever even tried to kiss me.

Cliff moved restlessly on the hard bench.

"Why do you suppose almost-grown men run around after a ball for no reason? It has to be misplaced competitiveness."

"Oh, nuts," Midge muttered loud enough for me to hear.

I kicked her sharply. "Don't be mean," I whispered.

After the game, when Midge and Cliff and Mike and I sat in a booth at The Barn, the local pizza place, Cliff asked Mike, "Why do you play basketball?"

Mike ran his hand through his shower-wet brown hair and narrowed his eyes. "What do you mean, why do I play?"

Cliff narrowed his black, black eyes back at Mike and pushed his black, black hair off his forehead. "Just what I said. Why do you play?"

Midge groaned and rested her head against the back of the booth. I leaned forward, interested in what Mike would answer.

Mike looked at Cliff and said simply, "Why *don't* you play?"

Cliff stared back at Mike, and then he laughed. Mike joined him and we all laughed together, enjoying the pizza and each other.

At that moment Timothy Thornton came in with Nancy Blackman, gorgeous

Nancy, cheerleader, voted Miss Popularity. As they passed our booth, Tim saw me and smiled. "Hi!" He stopped and looked at Mike with admiration. "That was a great game you played. You sure know how to make those baskets."

Mike looked a little embarrassed, but he smiled back at Tim. "Thanks," he mumbled.

Nancy put her arm through Tim's, and I could see she was trying to edge him away from the table. He put a hand over hers, said, "See you around," and walked away.

I stared at the back of his blond head. I couldn't take my eyes off it, until I felt Midge's foot on top of mine under the table. I looked up and saw the understanding and empathy on her face, and imperceptibly I shook my head to clear away the dreams.

As I climbed the stairs to my room later that night, I felt sad and puzzled. As I passed Grandma's room I saw a light coming from her slightly opened door. Knocking softly, I whispered, "Grandma?"

She whispered back, "Come in, Juliet."

She was in bed, her glasses on the edge of her nose, and *The New York Times* spread out all around her. She patted the blankets next to her, and I went over and curled up against her.

"Why, Grandma? Why?"

"Why what, Juliet?"

"Why does one boy in the world seem so . . . so exceptional and all the others seem so ordinary?"

She took her glasses off and laid her cheek against the top of my head. "Well, I guess you'd call it chemistry. Either it exists or it doesn't. You can't force it or pretend."

"Too bad I can't feel chemical about Mike or Cliff instead of —" I stopped short.

Grandma looked at me questioningly. "Is there a boy you do feel chemical about?"

I curled closer to Grandma. "I love you, Grandma."

"I love you, too, Juli. But — what?"

"But I don't want to talk about it, if you don't mind."

Grandma smiled and pushed me away from her. She looked at me with what I felt was all the wisdom in the world. "Don't ever apologize for wanting to keep some feelings private. It's your right to do so. Now go to bed. It's late."

She kissed my cheek, and I tiptoed down the hall to my room, not wanting to wake my mother. In bed I thought

24

about what Grandma had said. But I knew it wasn't just chemistry I felt toward Tim. There was a sweetness about him, a niceness, that touched me. He was always so gracious, like stopping to tell Mike how good he was. Mike was nice, too, but I didn't want to sit and stare at him, or reach out and touch his hand, and I didn't look forward to something as simple as just being in the same room with him. And Cliff was, well, interesting. Both of them, Mike and Cliff, were good-looking, too, in their own way.

I sighed and turned over on my side, wishing, strangely, that they would all go away.

The next thing I was aware of was my mother's hand on my shoulder. She shook me gently as she said, "Juliet, Mike is on the phone."

I opened my eyes to a room filled with sunshine and asked, "What time is it?"

"Nine."

I burrowed deeper under the covers and muttered, "Ugh."

Mother said with a faint tone of annoyance, "Juliet, are you coming to the phone or not? He wants to go bike-riding."

I sat up and slipped my feet into a pair of orange, woolly slippers and with my eyes half-closed went to the phone that was on a table in the hall between the bedrooms. It had a long cord on it and it could be dragged into any room on the floor for privacy, but Mike and I never had any private things to say to each other, so I stood in the hall, shivering slightly.

"Hi, Mike."

"Hey, want to ride up into the hills?"

I shivered again. "How cold is it out?"

He laughed. "You'll warm up riding. Come on. I'll pick you up at eleven."

I liked the warm, friendly sound of his voice, so I said, "Okay. See you at eleven."

I walked downstairs to the kitchen, where my mother was drinking a cup of coffee. I poured a glass of orange juice and sat next to her at the table. Grandma came in and said, "What do you want for breakfast?"

Mother's mouth tightened slightly. "Ma, she can make her own breakfast. She's a big girl."

Grandma went on taking eggs from the refrigerator, ignoring Mother. "I like to do it for her. What's the harm?"

Mother shrugged. "None, I guess. You just spoil her."

It was an old argument and I listened with amusement, turning my head from one to the other as they sparred back and forth, feeling as if I was at a tennis match I had seen played before.

Grandma looked at Mother with mild condescension. "There isn't a spoiled bone in Juli's body. You know it. Juli, scrambled or fried?"

"Bones or eggs?"

Grandma shook her head and began scrambling eggs without waiting for my answer.

I dressed as warmly as I could and still move my arms and legs, and was ready when Mike stopped by. We rode up into the hills behind our city, not talking much as we pedaled. We kept a steady pace, and I felt comfortable and not even cold. Mike and I enjoyed doing things like that together — biking, bowling, swimming in the summer. We had a companionable relationship mostly based on the sports we shared. Our heads were usually in different places.

After riding for about an hour, we stopped high above town and sat on a hill overlooking the center of the city. Mike pulled out two candy bars and handed me one.

"Mmm," I said. "Good idea, except our teeth will rot instantly."

"I don't worry about that," Mike said, grinning, and showing me his even, dazzling white teeth.

He bit into the candy and said, "You know, you ride pretty good for a girl. You keep up with me just fine."

"You are the most chauvinist person I know. I don't even think you mean things like that. You just say them to irritate me."

He looked at me blankly. "You mean because I say you're a good sportsman, that's bad?"

I stared at him silently.

"Okay. Okay. Sportsperson. Sportswoman. Whatever you want."

"Thanks," I muttered, and then asked, "Do you know that Oliver Ellison is moving back to town?"

Mike twisted around and said, "Oliver? Oh, yeah, he was the kid who wrote poetry."

I tested Mike carefully. "What's wrong with writing poetry? I write it often."

"Do you really? You never told me that." Mike looked at me strangely.

"You never asked," I answered. "If a

person could earn a living writing poetry, that's what I'd like to do when I'm — I guess you'd call it grown-up."

"How about that," Mike murmured softly.

"Do you think it's so peculiar?" There was a sharp edge to my voice.

Mike looked at me with a puzzled expression. "No. I kind of envy you and that Oliver kid."

Now I was the puzzled one. "Why? I never thought you'd feel that way."

Mike looked down at his big hands. The hands that could hold a basketball with total assurance. "Well," he said, "I'm not much in the head department. It's tough for me to study, to get decent marks on tests, to remember what I *have* studied. And that comes easy to you."

I touched his hand very lightly. "Mike, there's nothing wrong with you. You just don't apply yourself. All you have to do is study a certain amount of time every day, take good notes, and —"

Mike laughed. "Organized Juli. You have it all figured out. Sensible Juli."

I looked away. "Not always," I said, briefly thinking of Timothy — golden Timothy.

"So if you can't make a living writing

poetry, what do you want to do?" Mike asked.

"I'm not sure. Maybe work on a newspaper or magazine. I'll bet you know what you want to do."

"I sure do. Play basketball as long as I can and then coach. It's all I want."

I punched his arm playfully. "Organized Mike. You have it all figured out."

He punched back. "You're right." He pulled me up by the arm. "Come on, let's go back and bowl."

Chapter Four

When I got home after bowling, I ran a steaming hot tub and dumped my favorite bubble bath into it. I was going to meet Cliff at the movies that night and wanted to be able to stay awake. I lay back in the tub, resting my head against the cool porcelain. I closed my eyes and felt my muscles relaxing. A knock at the door made me jump.

"Juli. It's me, Barb. Can I come in?"

"Sure. Just keep the cold air out."

Barbara came in and sat on the closed seat of the john, which was at the foot of the tub. She dipped a finger in the bubbles and said, "I'm sorry if I was nasty at dinner last night. I just get so jealous because you can do everything you want, and I can't do anything."

I looked at Barbara's sweet face and her big, brown eyes that were filled with confusion. "That's not true, Barb. It's only when it comes to Alfie that Mom cracks down a little. I don't have an Alfie, so I don't have the problem."

Barb sighed softly. "Well, maybe Oliver . . ."

I moved in the tub suddenly, spilling water over the edge. "Why is everyone acting as if Oliver is a knight come to Dellwood? He's just Oliver. He's not —"

Another knock at the bathroom door stopped me. "Juli. Can I come in? It's Mother."

"Come on in. Everyone else is."

My mother opened the door and looked surprised at seeing Barbara sitting with me. "I'm sorry. Am I interrupting something?"

Barb and I both shook our heads, and Mother said with enthusiasm, "I just spoke to Eve Ellison. They're here, and coming to dinner tomorrow night. I thought you'd like to know." She looked at me somewhat conspiratorially.

"Fine," I muttered.

Mother looked annoyed. "You don't seem very pleased. I thought you'd like Oliver coming back. Sometimes I don't understand either of you at all."

She turned to the door and started to open it, when Barbara said plaintively, "Why does this happen so much now?"

Mother turned back to her. "Why does what happen?"

Barbara's voice sounded funny, as if she were about to cry. "Why do we argue so much? We didn't used to."

I slipped farther under the bubbles and said, "She's right, Mom. Why do we?"

Mother leaned against the door wearily. Her blue eyes looked over our heads. "We used to have another person here. You had a father. I had a husband, a friend. I think we all miss him a lot, and our fuses are short."

Barb twisted a strand of her long hair. "It's six years since he died. Shouldn't we be used to it by now?"

Mother stroked Barbara's head. "Six years isn't so long to adjust to something like that."

I slid even further down in the warm water. "That's why we jump all over each other?"

She smiled at me thoughtfully. "I don't know, Juliet. I just said maybe. Think about it if you feel like it."

Mother turned back to the door. "Grandma and I have to start figuring out dinner for tomorrow night, right now. See you."

Barbara and I were silent for a few minutes, both of us mulling over what Mother had said. Then I said:

"The Sweeping up the Heart
And putting Love away
We shall not want to use again
Until Eternity."

"What was that?" Barbara asked.

"Something Emily wrote."

"Emily who?"

I glared at Barbara. "You're really almost illiterate. Emily Dickinson."

Barbara stood up. "I thought you were talking about a friend or something."

"I was. She's my friend."

Barbara smiled. "You're nuts." But her voice was filled with warmth. "Well, this friend here is telling you you'd better get out of the tub or you'll look like a raisin."

"Sometimes I feel more like a prune."

Barbara looked at me from the doorway. "You're not so bad."

* * *

After the movie that night, Cliff and I went to The Barn. I was feeling distracted, and during a good part of the movie had been thinking about what my mother had said while we had all been in the bathroom.

"You're quiet," Cliff muttered while we waited for our hamburgers. "Something bothering you?"

I told him about my conversation with Mother. "Do you think that's true? That we're still reacting to my father's death?"

Cliff rearranged the silverware on the table. "I don't know. What do *you* think?"

I was annoyed at him and showed it. "What are you doing, practicing being a psychiatrist? 'What do *you* think?' If I knew, I wouldn't be asking you."

"Well," Cliff answered firmly, "you have to figure things like that out for yourself. You have to think about it."

I pushed some hair off my cheek. "Sometimes I think we think too much."

Cliff shook his head vigorously. "You can never know too much about how you feel about things."

I decided to change the subject. "Oliver Ellison is back in town. He and his folks are coming for dinner tomorrow night. Remember him?"

"Sure. He's the kid who wrote poetry."

"How come no one seems to remember anything else about Oliver except that he wrote poetry? You'd think it was some kind of awful scar."

Cliff raised his eyebrows. "Who said anything about a scar? I just mentioned that he wrote poetry. I wonder if he's changed much."

I smiled. "So do I. I guess everyone changes in four years. I certainly hope I have."

I spent extra time getting dressed that Sunday. I brushed my hair until shiny, short ends clung to my cheeks and forehead. I put on lip gloss and a little blush and wore a skirt and a bright yellow sweater.

When I went downstairs, my hands were damp and a pulse was fluttering at the side of my neck. The Ellisons were all in the living room. I gasped at my first look at Oliver.

He *had* changed ... and he hadn't.

He had grown at least seven inches and was now a lot taller than I. He had lost weight and was pleasantly lanky. But his hair still hung almost over his soft gray eyes, and he still didn't know what to do with his hands and feet.

We moved toward each other, smiling. But suddenly we stood still. We certainly weren't going to kiss and it was ridiculous to shake hands. Then we were grabbing each other's arms and wrists, and laughing, and mumbling clichés all at the same time.

"You've grown so," I said. "Oh no, I can't believe I'm saying that. I sound like somebody's great-aunt."

Oliver laughed. "You look exactly the same."

"I do? I don't want to. I must have changed somewhat in four years."

Oliver moved away and looked at me closely. "Sure you have. You're taller, too, and your hair is shorter."

"Don't I look more mature? Wiser? Worldier?"

Oliver laughed again. "Hell, Juli, I'm not doing a character analysis; I'm just giving you a spur of the moment impression."

Grandma had outdone herself with dinner, stuffing cabbage leaves with meat and rice, rolling them up tightly, and cooking them in succulent sauerkraut. Mother had baked a big cheesecake. We all talked practically at the same time throughout dinner, catching up on who had done what when. Mr. Ellison was going to be the top salesman with a new company in town, and Mrs. Ellison was opening a boutique for budget-conscious women — namely everyone.

After dinner, Oliver and I went up to my room so we could talk by ourselves. I sat on the floor and watched him carefully looking at the books on the shelves. He'd pick one out, look through it, nod his head, and put it back, going on to another.

He looked at the poetry shelf more carefully than all the others. "Anne Sexton, Sylvia Plath, Dickinson, Millay. No men, just women. How come? Got something against men poets?"

I shook my head. "No. I like a lot of them. It's just that women say something to me that I can connect with more. What about you? Still writing?"

Oliver sat next to me on the floor. "No. I gave all that up. Who can earn a living being a poet? I'm studying journalism, going in for newspaper work. You? Still writing?"

"Yes, some."

"I'd like to see something."

I looked down at my hands nervously. "I couldn't. It isn't very good."

Oliver touched my shoulder lightly. "You used to show me everything you wrote. Remember? It didn't matter if it was good or not."

Suddenly, the four years Oliver had been gone didn't mean anything. He was Oliver, my good friend, and I got up and found the last poem I had written.

I gave it to him silently and he read it silently.

> Hands that warm mine with a
>   gentle touch
> Bring belief. Yes, a receptive
>   heart is weak.
> Again I dream of everlasting love
>   and such,
> Knowing well that time will bring
>   sighs and tears,
> But even oft-scarred hearts are
>   pioneers.

He lifted his eyes from the page and looked out of the window. "It's good. Who is it about?"

"Someone who doesn't know I'm alive, and never will."

Oliver touched my hand gently. "Then he's a dope."

Chapter Five

And that's how the next six weeks went. I
bowled with Mike. I examined motiva-
tion, feelings, and where-were-we-all-
going with Cliff. I talked poetry and books
and the world with Oliver.

I wasn't unhappy, but I wasn't exactly
happy either. I liked being with the three
boys; I enjoyed myself with them, but if I
didn't see one of them for a few days I
really didn't miss him. In school, it was
Timothy that I was almost unconsciously
looking for all the time. And when I saw
that bright, shining head in the midst of
all the nondescript ones, I felt a glow, an
inner smile. When he looked at me or

talked to me, no matter how briefly, I felt a happy pain.

One night, Oliver and I went to a party given by Faith Davis, one of the girls in the Drama Club. It was a spur of the moment thing and to make it more fun, Faith had invited a motley group of kids, someone for everyone. I was having a good time talking to drama girls, sports fans, and chorus tenors, when I saw Timothy come in with Deedee Bennett. Deedee had been Prom Queen the year before and always walked as if she still wore the crown on her head — beautifully and elegantly.

I watched Tim getting her a Coke, dancing with her, and bending his head to hear her when she talked, and I could feel my teeth clenching and my jaw tightening. I was hardly aware of him walking across the room until I heard his voice.

"Juli, would you like to dance?"

I looked up and opened my mouth enough to say, "Sure."

That's what I mean about Tim's always being nice and thoughtful.

Because we had grown up together, gone to school together, he would always dance with me once at every party. Once — that was all. The music was slow, and when he put his arm around me and brought me close to him, I felt tears coming to my eyes. I didn't really even know why. I just felt sad and lonely.

He pressed his cheek against mine, and I could smell the faint odor of his aftershave lotion and feel the scratchy softness of his skin. He looked down at me and said, "You always were a great dancer."

"Really?"

He laughed. "Didn't anyone ever tell you?"

I was embarrassed and looked away. "Maybe I never listened before."

I guess that was the high point of the month for me.

Then one day in the middle of March, I was in the kitchen getting ready to set the table for dinner. Barbara was helping me, and Grandma was upstairs taking a bath. I remember it all as if time had stopped for a moment, or a camera had taken an instant snapshot. The phone rang and I picked it up with one hand, while I rummaged in a kitchen cabinet for napkins with the other.

"Hello," I said automatically.

"Juliet?" A fluid male voice asked.

"Yes?"

Then the voice said softly:

43

"Did my heart love till now?
Forswear it, sight!
For I ne'er saw true beauty till this night."

I was dumbstruck, astounded. "Who is this?" I asked.

The voice answered gently, "Someone who cares about you."

There was a soft click as the caller hung up.

I sat down in the nearest chair and could feel my legs shaking and a faint pounding in my head. Barbara looked at me and then came over and put her hand on my shoulder. "What's wrong? You're so pale."

I looked up at her and said breathlessly, "A man just called and quoted some lines from *Romeo and Juliet* to me."

"Obscene lines?" she asked.

That snapped me back to reality. "You really *are* illiterate. What could be obscene about *Romeo and Juliet?*"

I quoted the lines to her, as well as I could remember them, and she shrugged. "How do you know they're from *Romeo and Juliet?*"

"I know because we're studying the play in English class. It's *Romeo and Juliet,* without a doubt."

Barbara patted my shoulder, trying to be reassuring. "Don't worry! It's just some nut who got our number out of the phone book. I mean, it doesn't mean a thing. Just forget about it. And don't tell Mom or Grandma — they'll call the police or something weird."

That night as I lay in bed, trying to fall asleep, I heard the voice in my head. The gentle voice whispered, "Did my heart love till now?" Then I heard Barbara saying, "It doesn't mean a thing," and I thought, *Doesn't it?*

The next day after school I lay on Midge's bed, gazing up at the white organdy canopy over it. Midge Roth is the only girl I know whose bed *should* have a white organdy canopy. It was right for the sweet image she presented to most of the world.

"And then he just said, 'Someone who cares about you,' and he hung up."

Midge sat motionless on a small, flow-ered-chintz chair near the bed. "That is absolutely astounding. Did you recognize the voice? I mean, did it remind you of anyone at all? *Think hard!*"

I sat up and rested my head on my

knees. "Well, somewhere there was something about it that reminded me of someone, but I can't pin it down. I've thought about it all day and I just can't hold on to anything. It's like waking up and knowing you've had a dream and yet you can't get even a small thread to start pulling on."

Midge came over and sat next to me. "Well, did it sound like he was nearby or far away?"

"Midge, for heaven's sake, I talk to my aunt in California a couple of times a month and she sounds like she's next door. It isn't the dawn of the telephone era, you know."

Midge reached for a pretzel that was in a bowl near her bed. She handed it to me and nibbled on one herself. "Maybe Barb is right. Maybe it's just some guy who gets a thrill out of calling strange girls. He'll probably never call again."

But she and Barbara were both wrong. A week after the first call, at exactly the same time, the phone rang.

After I said hello, the same lovely, tender voice said:

"It is my lady; O, it is my love!
    O that she knew she were!"

This time I said with more firmness, "Who *is* this?"

And he answered just as he had the week before, "Someone who cares about you," and hung up.

Barbara was in her room, and I went up to her and sat down on the floor with my back against the wall. "He called again."

She didn't ask who. She knew. "Wow! What did he say this time?"

I repeated the lines word for word.

Barbara joined me on the floor and picked at little pieces of lint on the carpet. "Well, if he's a nut, at least he's an educated nut. I mean you haven't got some garden variety creep calling you."

"He's not a creep. I know it. He's . . . he's —"

"He's what?" Barbara asked impatiently.

"I don't know, but I do know he's not scary. He's a nice person."

My grandmother had gone downtown to meet a friend for dinner, and Mother was going shopping after work, so Midge was coming over to have dinner with us. When she arrived, Barbara and I were in the kitchen making spaghetti. I quickly filled her in and she made small sounds of amazement as she set the kitchen table.

Barbara put Grandma's thick meat sauce in a pan and said thoughtfully,

"Okay. You said you're studying *Romeo and Juliet* in English. Maybe it's some guy in your class who's making funnies. Does that seem possible? Is there someone who bugs you or jokes or teases? *Something?*"

I shook a fork, with a strand of spaghetti twisted around it, at Barb. "Everyone jokes or teases or bugs. If that meant something, it could be any boy in the class."

Midge looked up from the spoons she was putting down and said, "It could be any boy in the class anyway. Couldn't it?"

"Not François Rémy. He barely speaks English."

We all laughed and suddenly I felt very happy. But just as I hadn't known why I felt sad when I danced with Tim, I didn't know why I felt happy now. Even so, I went to the kitchen cabinet and took out two wine glasses and an open bottle of red wine.

"Since I am such a femme fatale and all of my English class is calling and reciting love poetry to me on the phone, I think you and I, Midge, should have a small glass of wine with our spaghetti."

I poured a little in the two glasses and set them on the table, as Barbara said indignantly, "What about me?"

48

"You're too young," I said in a miserably superior tone. "Mother lets me have a little sometimes, but not you, and you know it. Have some grape juice."

That night as I washed my face, I looked into the mirror over the sink at the girl reflected there. I stared hard at her until I had stepped out of myself and could see the girl in the mirror as a separate person — a girl named Juliet Gibson, who had hazel eyes that were now wide and dilated, set in a pale, delicate face with high cheekbones and a curved pink mouth.

"Someone loves you," I whispered to the girl.

When I got into bed and pulled my fluffy green comforter up to my chin, I thought, *Who is it?* I went over every boy in English class, and then came to the unthinkable: *Oliver? Cliff? Mike?*

Chapter Six

The next day, as I was sitting in my English class, I looked around the room and examined each boy. I had just about decided that I was paranoid when I noticed Davey Feiner staring at me, his brown eyes wide and sheeplike. I stared back at him thinking, *Davey?*

But that was impossible. Davey Feiner was shy to the point of being almost mute. If he had to speak to a female, even a female teacher, he blushed a brilliant red. Finally I smiled at him, very slightly, very gently. To my stunned amazement, he smiled back at me, shyly, sweetly. I averted my eyes quickly and focused them and my total attention on the teacher.

At the end of the day, I said to Midge, "I think it's Davey Feiner."

Midge looked at me as if I had suggested it was Mick Jagger. "You're crazy. Davey Feiner barely speaks, much less makes passionate declarations of love."

I pulled my books closer to my chest as we walked through the hall to the exit doors. "Well, maybe he does better on the phone than he does in person."

Midge shook her head, refusing to believe it. "If it's Davey Feiner, you are not only a modern-day love object, you're also an emotional cure-all."

As we walked home, I looked at every boy we passed with an appraising eye and noticed Midge doing the same thing.

I laughed at her as she poked me when a boy on a bike almost ran me down. "You're worse than I am. Come on, I have to stop at the supermarket to pick up some things for Grandma. Want to come along?"

"No, but I will, just to avoid going home and starting the math assignment."

In the market, when I reached the checkout counter, I piled the food up next to the register. A pair of hands reached into my ba‌‌‌et and helped pull the stuff out. I looked up into the eyes of the boy who worked there in the afternoons.

"Hi, gorgeous."

He'd never spoken to me before. Why now?

"Hi," I whispered shyly, and watched him carefully as he rang up every item. He had a poetic look about him, in spite of his flaming red hair and white coat.

As Midge and I left the store, I said, "The checkout boy said 'Hi, gorgeous' to me."

"Did he really? He never talks to anyone. He's Mister Unfriendly. Do you suppose —"

I hiked up the bag of groceries and interrupted, "I can't do this anymore. I'll go crazy if I think every boy or man I meet is the caller."

Midge took a box of cookies from the top of the bag and opened it, taking out a chocolate cream sandwich. "Well, someone is doing it, so anyone is possible — even Mister Unfriendly. Maybe someone like him is *more* likely."

The next week, at the same time as the other two calls, the third one came. I knew the moment the phone rang who it was and this time there was a softness in my voice as I answered.

"Hello," I said almost musically.

     "Ah, dear Juliet;
     Why art thou yet so fair?"

I grasped the receiver tighter, pressing it against my cheek. "Who are you? Why won't you tell me? Please."

I heard a soft click, as if the phone had been replaced with a caress.

When I looked up, Barbara was standing next to me. "Him?"

I nodded my head. She looked troubled. "Maybe you should tell Mother."

"Why? Whoever it is hasn't done anything bad or scary."

Barbara shivered slightly. "I know, but it's just so strange."

I disagreed. "If you heard his voice, you'd know it isn't strange or menacing or frightening. It's . . . it's lovely."

That night at dinner I felt as if I were in a different place than my own home, my own dining room, with my own family. I pushed the food around on my plate and every now and then lifted a forkful to my mouth. I felt someone staring at me and saw Mother's blue, blue eyes peering at me.

53

"Are you all right?" she asked.

"Sure. Why?"

She lifted a glass of water and shrugged. "You just seem peculiar."

"I'm fine. Really." But I knew she wasn't satisfied.

Neither was Grandma. As we did the dishes, she said, "Your mother is right. Only it's been a couple of weeks that you've seemed peculiar."

I concentrated on drying a pot while I asked, "Why didn't you say anything before?"

Grandma concentrated just as hard on wiping the salad bowl and said casually, "I figured if you wanted to tell me anything you would. And if you didn't, you wouldn't."

I set the pot down and put my arms around Grandma's waist. "It's nothing, Gram — really."

"I doubt that, but when you're ready, you'll tell me. Whatever it is, it isn't bad."

I rested my cheek against hers. "How do you know?"

"From the look on your face."

The next afternoon as we left school, Midge said, "Ingels is having a sale on sweaters. Want to go look?"

"Sure, I still have some Christmas money left. I might even buy something."

"That should make Mr. Ingels happy," Midge joked.

When we got to the sportswear department, there were three tables piled high with sweaters. Midge and I poked through them all.

Midge held one up. "This looks like you. Want to try it on?"

It was a well-made, sturdy, beige Shetland. The kind of sweater that would last forever. I shook my head no and said, "I think I'll try this one on."

I held up a pale pink, fluffy pullover with short puffy sleeves. It was made of a combination of wools, including angora, so it had a soft, wispy, romantic look. Midge raised her eyebrows in surprise.

"It's beautiful. But I've never seen you wear anything like that."

"I know," I said, rubbing my cheek against the sweater. "I thought just for a change."

Midge touched the sweater, too. "You sure surprise me, but try it on."

We went into a tiny dressing room together and Midge held my coat, book bag, and the sensible green sweater I'd been wearing, while I put on the pink sweater,

55

struggling in the limited amount of space we had. I looked in the mirror and saw a girl whose eyes were sparkling, whose cheeks reflected the delicate pink of the sweater, and whose lips were smiling slightly, mysteriously.

"You look great," Midge said. "Buy it, without a doubt. How much is it?" She picked up the price tag and whistled softly. "Have you looked at the price?"

"If it's under the national debt, I'm buying it."

"Well it's not quite that much so you're safe." Midge handed me back my clothes. "I'll wait for you outside, before we're both asphyxiated in here."

The next morning I put on the sweater to wear to school. It looked as good as it had the day before, and I tried to think of what to wear with it. I wanted to put on a new, pleated gray skirt I had, but I was afraid I would look too different — that I'd stand out like the "after" in a before-and-after ad — so I pulled on a pair of old jeans. I went into the bathroom to comb my hair and tried not to look at Barbara who was brushing her teeth.

She spit into the sink and glanced at me, squinting her eyes. "Hey, that's a great sweater. When did you get it?"

"Yesterday," I said casually, and started brushing my hair.

She looked me up and down and said, "Don't you think it would look better with your new gray skirt?"

I glared at her. "No, I don't. I'm wearing what I want to wear. *If* you don't mind."

She shrugged and walked out of the bathroom. "Okay. Okay."

In the kitchen, Grandma looked up from the stove. "Hmmm. Nice. Don't you think you should wear your new gray skirt with that?"

I was never cranky with Grandma, or hardly ever, but I snapped. "No! I like just what I have on."

Mother rushed into the kitchen. "I'm late," she mumbled, and grabbed the orange juice. She looked at me and said, "Don't you think —"

I shouted at her, "No! I don't think."

She glared at me with her mouth slightly open. "What's with you? All I was going to ask was —"

"I know what you were going to ask and the answer is —"

Mother set her glass down hard, the juice slushing onto the table. "I was going to say, 'Don't you think it would be nice if

57

you met me downtown for dinner to-night?' " She looked at Barbara. "You and I will do it next week."

I mopped at the orange juice with my napkin and said, "I'm sorry. I thought . . . Sure I'd like to meet you tonight."

Mother got up from the table and put her glass in the sink. "Good. Try to be a little cheerier. I'll see you at The Pub at six."

In school nobody paid much attention to me, but I was constantly aware of the soft wool on my arms and back. It made me feel different, a little more like the kind of girl a boy might call and quote poetry to. I felt apart from the rest of the class, as if something was happening to me that wasn't happening to anyone else I knew. It was a nice feeling, but it fright-ened me, too.

Oliver, who was in my history class, smiled at me when I came into the room and raised his eyebrows in appreciation. Oliver always noticed things other people were never aware of. After class, he came over to me and brushed his hand against my shoulder. "Feels nice. So do you."

I heard the voice, *"Why art thou yet so fair?"* and for one brief moment I looked directly into Oliver's eyes and said, "Thank you." Then, though I don't think I'd ever blushed in my life, I felt a warmth in my cheeks and looked away in-embarrassment.

Oliver stared at me hard and, almost as if he didn't know he was going to say it, asked, "How about a movie Friday night?"

"Sure. Fine."

He started to the door and then turned back. "I'll pick you up at seven." Then he went into the hall.

Oliver had *never* picked me up to go to a movie. We always met at the theater. *Always.* I kept looking at the door Oliver had gone through. *Oliver?* I thought. He could be the one. He liked poetry. He had written poetry. He was studying *Romeo and Juliet. Oliver?*

As I left the classroom, Timothy was coming in. We passed each other and he smiled that joyous smile of his. "Hi, Juli." He tossed it over his shoulder as he went to his seat. I could have had on a flour sack for all he noticed.

The Pub attracted all kinds of people. Families came in for dinner, school kids came in for hamburgers, and older people came in because there was no jukebox. At dinner time, there were candles on the red-checkered tablecloths and soft canned

59

music. The candle on our table threw a pale, wavering light on Mother's face, making her skin look like the Chinese ivory parchments I'd seen in a museum. When she smiled at me, I was startled as always by the open, childlike expression in her eyes. The blue-gray smudges seemed so out of place.

"Tired?" I asked.

She shook her head. "Worried, more than tired. There never seems to be enough time, enough money. But don't *you* worry. One of us is enough."

"I wish I could help more."

"You help enough. You've got your school-work, and I know you're up late too many nights writing whatever it is you write in your room. It used to be poetry. Is it still?"

When she asked me, I realized with a sharp needle of pain that we had grown far apart; that we didn't have the long talks we used to; that I didn't run to show her every new poem as I used to; that she really didn't know what was in my head and I didn't know what was in hers. And I also realized that I missed the closeness; as much as I loved Grandma and thrived in her warmth, she wasn't my mother.

"Yes," I answered. "It's still poetry."

She nodded her head and went on. "And you help Grandma a lot, too. You've got enough to do. Grandma thinks you have *too* much to do."

I smiled. "She would feel that way." The love I felt for Grandma Lang flowed into my words.

Mother looked down at her drink and twisted the swizzle stick in it. "You feel very close to her, don't you? I mean, closer than to me?"

I was uneasy at the turn the conversation had taken, but I wanted to answer my mother. "I feel close to her in different ways than I feel close to you. I mean ... I know she always approves of me, and ..."

Mother touched my hand. "It's okay, Juli. It really is. It can't hurt to have someone in your life who thinks you're perfect."

I saw that she was smiling broadly, and I had to laugh. But then I looked over her head and saw Timothy coming in with Deedee. His arm was around her shoulders, and I could picture the hand that rested lightly on her red sweater. I knew the long fingers, the clean nails that were cut straight across, and the wide watchband that circled his wrist. When I looked back at Mother she was watching me.

"So that's the way it is," she said.

I felt my body tightening, and I tried to control my voice. "How *what* is?"

"Juli, I couldn't mistake that look. You like Timothy."

My hands were clenched under the table, and I felt my thumb pressing hard into a knuckle. "Of course, I like him. We practically grew up together."

Mother picked up her drink and sipped it. "Okay. Okay. You don't have to say anything. But I didn't mean 'like' in that way. I mean *really* like."

For the rest of the meal we talked about politics and poetry and life. I felt connected to her as we sat and ate and talked, almost the way I used to. I relaxed and sensed her unwinding. I almost told her about the caller, more to prolong the intimacy we were feeling than to share the boy or man — whatever he was — with her. But something stopped me, a protectiveness, a drawing back. I wasn't sure which.

Chapter Seven

As I dressed on Friday night, my mind was half on Oliver and half on the mysterious caller. It had been over three weeks since the first call, and each week there had been another one. I was beginning to count on them in some funny way. But I wasn't sure what I counted on them for. Excitement, yes; something unusual in my life, yes; but it was more than that. I was more aware of being a female-type person, I guess. My father had always made me feel like a girl. He had complimented me on the way I looked, when I knew I was all elbows and knees and awkwardness. He had made me feel graceful and pretty. Cer-

63

tainly, Grandma thought I was attractive; as a matter of fact, Grandma thought I was gorgeous. But that was because she was Grandma. Mother didn't put that much importance on how I looked, maybe because she was so busy and preoccupied now that she didn't have the emotional energy to think about how *she* looked. She was always beautiful, anyway.

Cliff and Mike never knew whether I had on jeans or a skirt or a barrel. And Oliver, well, Oliver mostly had his head in a book, except for moments like the other day.

Now I found myself thinking, *"Why art thou yet so fair?"*

My caller thought I was "fair." I had never thought of myself, or anyone else I knew, as fair. It was such a lovely, evocative word.

I reached for my old jeans and threw them on the floor. I pulled my new skirt out of the closet and found a pale blue cotton shirt that didn't need ironing. I knotted a red scarf around my neck, put on a tiny bit of eyeshadow, and sprayed on some cologne. As I looked in the mirror I whispered to the Juli I saw, "Mirror, mirror on the wall, who is the fairest of them all?"

I laughed as I ran down the stairs, thinking, *You are a nut.* But I didn't feel like a nut. I just felt good.

When Oliver came, it was the same as always. Coming to the house to pick me up didn't make any difference. He was still Oliver. He didn't fling his jacket down for me to walk on or anything like that. We talked to my mother for a while and then I put my coat on. He held the door open for me and jokingly bowed slightly as I went through. "Ah, dear Juliet," he said as I stepped outside. My breath caught in my throat and I spun around to look at him, examining his face closely. Oliver wrinkled up his forehead. "What's up?"

"Why did you say that?"

"Say what? All I said was 'dear Juliet.' That is your name, isn't it? You're weird tonight." He looked away quickly.

I was terribly embarrassed for a moment. "I'm sorry," I mumbled. There was no sense in trying to explain. Oliver looked perfectly innocent, and yet . . .

At the movie, I went over what had happened at home — or hadn't happened. Was I imagining things, or had Oliver been trying to tell me something? I turned to look at him and found him watching me. He leaned over and whispered, "You smell good." In the dark I could see him smile at me, and then he took my hand and held it.

I was so surprised that I just let my hand lie limply in his. He whispered to me again. "You're supposed to close your fingers around mine. That's what holding hands is."

I tried hard not to laugh out loud, and circled my fingers around his. The palm of his hand was warm and smooth, with just the beginnings of a callus under his middle finger. It was the first time Oliver had ever touched me in any personal way. I liked the way his hand felt, and I liked the way *I* felt holding it. It was a new experience for me to think of Oliver in any way but as a dear friend. Now I wondered again, *Was it Oliver?*

After the movie, Oliver seemed strange — strained. I had never felt awkward with him, but now I did, because he was awkward with me. Though I had felt like a different Juli in the movie theater, I was still the *me* Juli, and I confronted Oliver openly. "What's wrong? You seem so uptight."

We were walking down the block to my house. The air was crisp and my breath made smoky blotches in the night. Oliver stopped walking and turned to me. "I don't know. You've never worn perfume before."

"*That's* what's making you act so peculiar? Perfume?"

Oliver started walking again, leaving me standing there. "I don't know. Something is different about you, and I don't know what it is. I mean, I know you so well, but now I'm thinking maybe I *don't* know you so well."

I was trying not to laugh at him. "It's wonderful what a little perfume can do," I joked, but I knew what he meant.

At home, Oliver and I went into the kitchen. He opened the refrigerator, pulled out the makings for a jumbo sandwich, and started piling cheese, ham, tomatoes, and pickles on bread. He was silent all the time he worked. I made tea, and as I poured the hot water over the tea leaves, I said, "Oliver, you're acting dumb."

He paused, one hand brandishing a knife to cut the sandwich. "You know why that is?"

"Why?"

"Because I *am* dumb. It's funny, but when I smelled that perfume I panicked. It was like the Juliet I knew was gone. The perfume was just a symbol. You know?" Oliver smiled sheepishly. "But here in the bright lights of the Gibson Café I can see you're the same Juli."

I was disappointed — "same Juli" indeed — but I ate my sandwich and let Oliver ramble on about how he felt being back in Dellwood. In my head I heard the voice, *"Why art thou yet so fair?"* Was it Oliver's?

When Oliver left, I went upstairs. My room was icy and I took my afghan and wrapped it around my shoulders. I sat on the floor and rested my head against the side of my bed. The room was dark with just the lights of passing cars gliding across the ceiling and walls. The house was still. Realistic, practical, logical Juliet whispered, "O Romeo, Romeo! Wherefore art thou Romeo?" Then I giggled, "Or, just as important, *who*fore art thou Romeo?"

Chapter Eight

The fourth call came the next week. It was a day early. Midge and I were studying in the kitchen when the phone rang. This time he asked, "Juliet?"

"Yes," I answered, beckoning wildly to Midge.

She ran over to me and placed her ear next to mine on the receiver. We barely breathed, so my caller wouldn't know anyone else was listening.

The warm, almost melodic voice said, "Heaven is here, where Juliet lives." He said again, "Juliet, I —" and then there was the click of the phone being hung up.

Midge leaned against me and said, "It's a real person!"

I pushed her away. "What do you mean, 'a real person?' Did you think I was making the whole thing up? Lying? Imagining? Crazy?"

Midge walked back to the table and sat down. "Of course I didn't think you were lying. For heaven's sake, Juli, calm down. I just meant hearing the voice makes him real."

I sat next to her and rested my head on the table. She touched my hair gently. "He didn't sound like anyone I know, and yet, you're right. There's something about the voice . . ."

I didn't know it was going to happen, but tears just started flowing down my cheeks. Midge took her hand away abruptly as she heard me sniffing and saw the teardrops dripping onto the table. "Juli, why? Why are you crying?" She sounded frightened.

"I don't know," I answered. But I did know, really. It was so frustrating to have this *person* in my life, calling, caring about me, and not knowing who he was or even how to find out. I wanted the calls, but I was angry because Romeo knew who *he* was and who *I* was, but *I* only

70

partially knew who *I* was. And I didn't have a clue who Romeo was. The more I thought about it, the more I cried.

Midge walked over to the counter and grabbed some Kleenex. She stuffed a wad in my hand and said firmly, "Juli, stop. Or at least tell me why you're crying."

I heard someone come into the kitchen and burrowed my head further into my arms.

"Juli," Grandma said. "Juli, dear, what's wrong?"

"Tell her," Midge said. "Tell her about it, Juli."

Grandma came to the table and took me firmly in her arms. "Tell me, Juli." There was a tone to her voice that I knew. It was her no-nonsense tone, and it was where Mother got hers from.

The whole story just poured out, from the first call to this last one. "He's nice, Grandma. I know it."

Grandma sat at the table with us. "Does your mother know?"

I shook my head. "Just Midge and Barbara . . . and him, the caller."

Grandma took my hand. "I think you should tell your mother. She's the one who should know."

"No, Grandma, please, not yet. Nothing

71

bad is happening. I don't want anyone else to know. I didn't even want you to know. Please!"

Grandma was silent for a moment and then said, "All right, but I don't know if I'm doing the right thing. Grandmas are one thing, mothers are another, and mothers are the ones who should have the troubles."

I looked startled, and Grandma laughed. "Don't worry, Juli. Anyway, the boy has good taste."

I wouldn't admit it to anyone, but I felt better knowing some adult was aware of what was going on. I felt grown-up and competent, but just to a point.

That call somehow triggered new feelings in me. Now I knew that it was not just a stupid joke, that whoever it was was someone who took me seriously and who had a certain amount of strange constancy. I thought of myself as a girl who didn't have to have a boyfriend to be content, even though I felt it might be exciting to have one, but this mysterious caller evoked new responses in me.

I had an awareness of my physical self that I hadn't had before. I walked through the halls at school standing straighter, aware of how my head sat on my neck. All the years of bike riding hadn't made me as aware of how my hips moved as did this new sense of my body. My arms swung more freely as I walked, too, and I felt I was getting to know a part of me I hadn't been that much in touch with before.

The night after the next call came, I looked in the mirror as I was getting ready to go to bed. I was startled by the girl I saw. I automatically trimmed my hair myself every few weeks. It kept me looking neat and well-groomed. But I hadn't cut a speck in five weeks, and my hair had grown enough so that little tendrils curled around my cheeks and forehead. They clung to my face, framing it softly and giving me a breathless, wild, carefree look. The ends of the curly wisps had a reddish glow to them, making my eyes look more golden. I liked what I saw, but I wasn't totally comfortable with that girl. "I have to get to know you better," I said to the reflection. "You interest me."

In the morning, the girl with the wild, tangled curls and the somewhat startled look was still there. When I went to my closet to find something to wear, I turned away discontentedly. Nothing I had was right, certainly not the man-tailored shirts, or the sensible Shetland sweaters, or the jeans that didn't fit well, and all of them in dull colors. It was also a fact that I didn't have the money to outfit the new Juliet, and I couldn't ask Mother for it. I put on a loose white sweater and faded, baggy jeans, knotted a scarf around my neck, and dug up an old red bracelet I had been given and never worn. They helped liven me up. On impulse I tied a wide leather sash around my waist.

As I walked to school I hoped Midge would meet me, and she did. She came running down the steps from her house and gasped, "I think we're late."

I didn't answer, just blurted out, "I need new clothes."

"What's wrong with what you have?" Midge asked.

"Everything is so boring and baggy and nothing-looking."

Midge stopped walking and brushed her hand over my hair. "Well, you sure aren't boring and baggy-looking. I've been wanting to tell you but I thought I'd make you self-conscious — you've been getting greater and greater looking. Nothing like having a mysterious caller to add something different to one's life."

"Midge, where am I going to get the money for just a couple of new things?"

We were at school and on our way to different classrooms. Midge ran down the hall and called over her shoulder, "I'll think about it. I'll see you after school."

I nodded and then remembered. "I can't. I promised Mike I'd help him with his English assignment."

I walked a few steps backward, watching to make sure Midge heard me. When she waved her hand, I started to turn around and crashed into Timothy. We grabbed each other as we teetered back and forth. I could almost feel the warmth of his fingers through my down coat and sweater. Even though I knew that was impossible, I liked the impossible feeling. He laughed and steadied himself. "Boy, Juli, you sure leave a guy breathless." He gave me a big grin and kept on walking.

I watched him. The easy stride, the blond hair that was standing up on the back of his head, the bright blue sweater that made his green eyes bluish. *Would it matter to you if you knew I had a caller? Would it make you see me?* I wondered.

* * *

Mike and I sat at the table in the dinette in his house, with papers covering the shiny Formica top. "What's so terrible about what you have to do for English?" I asked.

Mike groaned. "I have to write a composition called, 'What High School Isn't Giving Me That I Want.' What a dumb idea that is."

I rearranged some of the papers and said, "Okay, tell you what, just write down some of the things you don't have in your life that you'd like. We'll take it from there."

Mike grabbed a piece of paper and smiled. "That's easy." He began to write furiously. I looked at the top of his brown head, but my thoughts were of a blond boy with green eyes, a boy who right now was probably with some beautiful, admiring girl at The Barn. Then I thought about the caller. I wondered what he looked like and what he liked to do. Did he read poetry, outside of *Romeo and Juliet*? Did he play basketball, like Mike? A soft smile parted my lips, and I pushed my hand through the hair that was curling on my forehead.

When I looked up, Mike was staring at me. "You're beautiful," he whispered.

76

"No," I whispered back. "Not really." I couldn't take my eyes away from his. They held me strangely riveted.

Then he leaned over and kissed me softly. He moved his head back slightly, put his hand under my chin, and kissed me again. This time not as gently. His mouth was warm. I couldn't help but kiss him back. When we drew apart, he pushed the paper he'd been writing on toward me. "Read it," he said.

At the top of his list he had written, A BEAUTIFUL GIRL. While I watched he added in parentheses, JULIET.

I jumped up out of the chair and grabbed my coat. "I have to go."

Mike took hold of my arms. "For heaven's sake, Juli, don't run. All I did was kiss you. Be sensible."

"I don't want to be sensible. I want to be *not* sensible for a while."

I struggled into my coat and Mike watched me, looking confused but happy. "I think I'm in love with you," he said. "I mean it."

I ran out of the door and down the street. *Is it Mike?* I thought. *Is Mike the caller?* My head was filled to utter confusion with Tim, the caller, Oliver holding my hand, and now Mike saying he loved me. I couldn't separate the images and the feelings. They excited me and they frightened me, too, and I wanted to be home — safe.

When I got home, I ran up to my room and lay down on the bed. I stared up and watched the shadows on the sloping ceiling grow darker, until the room had no light left in it. The doorknob turned, and Mother stood next to my bed.

"Don't you feel well?" she asked.

"I guess I'm all right."

She started to turn away and said, "Then come down to dinner."

I curled up into a tight ball and murmured, "I don't really want any dinner."

I felt the bed sink slightly as she sat down on the edge of it. "Juli, stop this nonsense. What's wrong?"

"I don't want to talk about it, Mom."

I couldn't see her face, but I knew that her lips were tightening with irritation. "You don't seem to want to talk to me about anything important anymore. Why?"

I turned away from her and looked out of the window next to my bed. "You always seem so busy. I guess I don't think you care much."

I felt her hand on my hair, brushing it back gently. "I care," she whispered. "I do. I know I'm preoccupied so much of the time, but it's just because I'm worried — and lonely so much of the time. But I care about you desperately."

I turned back to her and reached up to touch her cheek. It was wet. When I felt her tears I threw myself in her arms and she held me close. My tears mingled with hers, and then we were laughing and clinging to each other. She kissed my cheek and snapped on the light. "Now will you tell me what's been going on? You've been different lately. Everything about you seems different — the way you walk, the tone of your voice, the way you hold your head."

I stood up and ran a comb through my hair. I smoothed down my sweater and looked at Mother. "Mom, not yet. Can we talk some other time? I'm just not ready."

Her eyes ran up and down me quickly. "I can't force you to talk about something you don't want to talk about, but I'm here when you want me." She stood back and looked at me even more closely. "I hope you're not going to scream when I say this, but everything about you looks different except your baggy clothes. Wouldn't you like to buy just a couple of new things that fit right? Please don't yell, just answer."

"Oh, Mom, can we afford it?"

She put her arm around my shoulders and hugged me. "Sure we can afford it. We'll just starve for a couple of weeks."

Sometimes it amazes me how things work out.

Chapter Nine

A few days later I went to Ingels after school, armed with my mother's charge card and a letter saying I was allowed to use it. I poked through racks of sweaters and skirts and blouses, feeling unsure and disoriented. I had always bought clothes more to cover my body and to be durable than to make me look and feel attractive. Now, I didn't know if I had any real concept of how I wanted to look.

I picked up a blouse with wide, red stripes, walked over to a full-length mirror, and held it up to me. As I raised my eyes I saw Deedee Bennett reflected in the shining glass. She was across the aisle, looking at me appraisingly. *Just what I need*, I thought. *Miss Glamour Facey giving me the eye.* I looked at the blouse, and then I met Deedee's eyes again.

She bent her head slightly to one side and shook her head no at me. She walked over and took the blouse out of my hands. "It isn't right for you," she said firmly. Then with a small smile, "I hope you don't mind, but you look sort of puzzled, and I'm pretty good when it comes to clothes."

She didn't wait for an answer but went over to a rack and pulled a blouse from it, hanger and all. She held it up against me and said, "See? This is better."

It was pale green with very narrow white stripes in it. It had a mandarin collar and long tight sleeves. It made my hair look redder and my eyes darker. It was stylish but soft and romantic at the same time. Our eyes met in the mirror again and we both smiled. *She's really nice*, I thought. *Not at all like I imagined.*

"You don't mind my leaping at you this way?" she asked with concern.

"No. I could use help desperately. I don't know what I want."

She squared her shoulders and took my arm. "I'm an expert. What else do you want to buy?" She didn't wait for me to answer, but went right on. "You have to have jeans that really fit you. With your figure, gorgeous and skinny, you should practically be poured into them. And you need soft colors for blouses and maybe some T-shirts — but stylish ones. I think you're kind of a chic, romantic type. You know, a combination of Cathy Earnshaw from *Wuthering Heights* and Diana Ross."

For the next hour we went frantically through the junior department, holding clothes up to me, trying things on, discarding and keeping things. When we left the store, I had a pair of tight jeans, a pale yellow skirt (would you believe, yellow? It would show every spot like crazy, and I didn't care), a frilly, Victorian, high-necked blouse, and a lilac T-shirt. As we walked out of the store, Deedee asked, "Do you have time to stop for a Coke?"

I hesitated and then said, "Sure." But as soon as we went into The Barn I became terrified. It was one thing to be busy shopping for clothes with Deedee, but what would we have to say to each other across a table? She was Deedee Bennett, Miss Glamour Facey, again, and we weren't in the same league.

As we walked to a table, I passed a mirror and stared briefly at my image — a girl who was standing up straight, walking with a slight swing; a girl with a mass of shining hair around a happily flushed face and excited, sparkling eyes.

"It is my love. O that she knew she were." I heard Romeo's voice and thought, *It's only Deedee Bennett, not Jane Fonda.*

We ordered Cokes and French fries and waited silently for them to come. I looked at Deedee and said shyly, "Thanks so much for helping me. It was really nice of you. I might have come home with a gorilla suit or something."

Deedee laughed. "I doubt it. You know, it's funny, I always thought you were a snob, but you're not at all."

I was astounded — more than astounded, stunned. "Me? *Me* a snob?"

"Sure," Deedee said. "You're always so aloof. I've tried to talk to you a couple of times, but you never seemed to notice."

"You did?" I asked. "I don't even remember. I've always felt intimidated by *you*. You're so beautiful and a prom queen, you know."

We both started to giggle and after that we talked about school and our favorite movies and exchanged all the gossip we knew about teachers. I waited for her to mention Tim, but she didn't. I wanted terribly to ask her if she was in love with him, but I couldn't, and I didn't want to spoil the good feelings between us. In a way, knowing she was nice made me feel even worse. No wonder Tim wanted to be with her. She wasn't only chic and beautiful — she was *nice*, too.

On the way home, I stopped at a phone booth and called Midge. "Meet me at home and stay for dinner. I have things to show you and wilder things to tell you. I'll be home in half an hour."

When Midge came, I took her up to my room and told her about the afternoon. "Funny," she said, "I always felt Deedee was a human being, that underneath all that gorgeousness was just a nice girl — one we never bothered to try to know. Poor Deedee."

"Come on," I said. "Let's not get carried away with sympathy for Deedee Bennett. She's still Miss Glamour Facey."

"Who's Miss Glamour Facey?" Barbara stood at the door, watching us.

"None of your business," I barked at her. "Do you always stand around eavesdropping?"

Barbara ignored me and came into the room. She poked at the packages on my bed. "What did you buy?"

I started wildly taking the new clothes out of the bags and holding them up to me. "Aren't they something?"

"For heaven's sake, try them on," Midge ordered. "The suspense is killing me."

One after the other, I put on the new things, while Midge and Barbara admired and oohed and ahhed at the appropriate moments.

Then I collapsed on the floor, exhausted from pulling clothes on and off, and looked up at Midge and Barb. Suddenly, all the fun was gone and I felt awful. "I think I hate myself," I said.

"Why?" they asked together.

I sat up and crossed my legs, yoga style. "Is this the kind of girl I am? I mean, a shallow, superficial girl who needs a male voice whispering sweet nothings on the phone to make her feel like a person?"

Barbara sighed. "You're getting more like Cliff all the time. Analyzing, analyzing."

But Midge was silent and thoughtful. Her sharp blue eyes were soft with reflection. "I don't think that's what this is about at all."

"No?" I asked bitterly. "I wasn't buying Victorian blouses and tight jeans or feeling like a pal to Deedee Bennett before Romeo started calling."

"Look, Juli," Midge said. "There are all kinds of different things that go into making a total girl. I mean, did you have any doubts that you were smart before Mr. Mysterious started calling?"

"No, of course not."

"Okay," Midge went on, gathering assurance as she spoke. "Why not? Because you've gotten top grades in school since third grade. So you had proof you were smart. Right? And you *felt* smart. Right?"

"Right," I answered. "So what's that got to do with anything?"

"Don't interrupt," Midge said firmly. "Now, have you felt you were a pretty good poet for a young person or at least an okay-type poet?"

"More okay-type for a young person than good," I said smiling.

"Right!" Midge said. "And why? Because you've won prizes in school. You've had things printed in the school literary magazine, and even the *Dellwood Times* has published a couple of your poems. So you had real proof you were talented, too. Right?"

"Right!" Barbara answered.

Midge ignored her and went on. "You've got lots of friends, so you've had to know you were kind and caring and interesting, or why else would you have friends?"

"When does the defense rest? I'm losing the point of all this," I said, still feeling unhappy.

Midge sat on the floor, facing me. "The thing you didn't have any assurance of was yourself as a girl who was attractive to boys in a boy-girl way. Cliff and Mike and Oliver have treated you like one of the boys, not a girl friend."

"That's for sure," I mumbled.

"Okay. So Romeo starts calling and all he does is give you some assurance where you don't have it. He tells you you're sexy and beautiful, and so you start acting and looking that way. It's really simple."

"She's right," Barbara said, joining us on the floor. "If I didn't have Alfie, I'd still feel like a little kid when it came to boy-girl things."

"In contrast to the mature adult you are now," I said.

"You know what I mean," Barbara said. And I did.

Midge took my hand. "You've had three

boys treating you like a teammate, and you've been yearning after one guy who treats you like a passing acquaintance, so you've acted like one — a teammate or a passing acquaintance."

"Who?" Barbara cried out. "Who are you yearning after? I never knew you yearned before. It's wonderful."

"Oh, Barbara, keep quiet," I said.

"Juliet," Midge said reassuringly, "You've always *felt* like a certain person and *acted* like that person. You're just finding out about another part of the same person, and the caller is what started that."

"Okay. So what does that say for Mike and Oliver? I'm the same me, but *they* are acting different."

"You're not the same at all. And they're responding to the sexy Juli who has never been around before."

Barbara's eyes narrowed. "*What* have you been doing, Juliet?"

I poked her in the ribs. "All sorts of evil things. Like wearing perfume and pink sweaters and letting my hair grow."

I turned back to Midge. "Maybe it's the boys who are superficial, then."

"Oh, nuts," Midge said. "They're normal, healthy boys, turned on by a beautiful girl, who on top of being beautiful is an old friend they *thought* they knew. It's very entrancing and intriguing."

I hugged Midge and stood up. "You're wonderful, and smart, and I hope you're right. I want you to be."

Chapter Ten

"Love goes toward love as schoolboys from their books."

It was at breakfast a few days later, when the phone rang. I picked it up absent-mindedly, expecting Midge or Alfie. Instead there was the low, lovely voice.

"It's morning," I said. "I mean, you've never called in the morning."

"Well, I —" the voice stopped suddenly. "Good-bye, Juliet."

"Wait," I cried. But the phone was dead. "Oh, you! Why don't you show your face?"

I went upstairs and sat on the edge of my bed aware of my hair curling on my forehead and my toes curling in the open sandals I had on. I stretched and stood up and touched my toes, closed my eyes, and shivered slightly. I put on the tight jeans and lilac T-shirt and went out into the late April morning. The sun was warming and the air was filled with the smell of newly budding trees and bushes. There was a softness to the breeze under the surface coolness. But I was mostly aware of the softness and the sun and the hazy, shimmering light. For no reason, I started to run down the block, faster and faster. I took a new route to school, instead of the familiar way. As I ran by Cliff's house, he came out of the door. "Wait," he yelled, just as I had done a little while before.

"I can't," I yelled back. "I have to run."

He panted up to me, trying to keep up with my long strides. Cliff was smart but definitely no athlete. "Juli, I want to talk to you. Stop!"

I stopped running and faced Cliff. He was trying to catch his breath unobtrusively. "There's a lecture at the university tonight — 'The Nature of Dreams.' Want to go with me?"

He was looking at me intently, and I knew he wanted to be with me, lecture or no. His black eyes held an expression of watchful, almost breathless waiting that had nothing to do with running. *Cliff, too,* I thought. Then, *Is it Cliff?*

"Sure. I'd love to go. What time?" I asked.

"I'll get my dad's car and pick you up at seven-thirty."

At lunch time, I sat with Midge and the three boys at a tiny table in the cafeteria. It was filled with empty milk cartons, trays of glutinous food, half-eaten apples, and candy wrappers. Mike pushed the things into one disgusting pile and said, "I'll see you tonight at the game. Right?"

I bit my lower lip, trying to think of what to say and then just blurted out, "I can't, Mike. I'm sorry. I forgot there was a game tonight and Cliff and I are going to a lecture at the university. I'm really sorry."

Mike clenched the fist that was resting on the table. "Well, you can go to a lecture some other time and come to the game tonight." He turned to Cliff and said through tight lips, "You know there's a game every Friday night."

Cliff stared at Mike coldly. "Yeah, and there's a lecture every Friday night, too. So what?"

Mike stood up. "Juliet always comes to the games."

Cliff stood up too and glowered at Mike. "Well, tonight she's going to a lecture, okay?"

Midge looked at me with raised eyebrows. "Don't you think you ought to say something definitive before they start knocking each other around? Or do you want them to fight over you?"

I looked at Midge with amazement. "Of course I don't want them to fight. Are you crazy?"

I stood up and put myself between them. "Look. This is all my fault. I forgot about the game."

Mike looked pained. "Not about you, Mike, just the game," I said quickly. "I did tell Cliff I'd go to the lecture, so just this week I will. Please, don't be angry."

Mike put his hand on my shoulder. "It's okay, Juli. Don't look so upset. How about a movie tomorrow night?"

"Sure. Sure," I said with relief. "Fine."

Mike looked at Cliff with a satisfied smirk on his face. "Enjoy your lecture." Then he walked away.

Oliver, who had sat sullenly through all this, muttered, "*I* was going to ask you to the movies."

Midge gathered her books together and smiled. "You have to move quickly, Oliver, if you want to have a date with Juliet. Get in line in plenty of time. You know the old saying: The early bird gets the girl."

"That's not quite right," Oliver said sullenly.

Midge pulled at me. "Come on, Juli. We're going to be late for class."

As we walked down the hall, Midge said, "Well, how does it feel being Cleopatra?"

I laughed sadly, as I watched Tim walking toward me with his arm around Deedee's shoulder. "One man's Cleopatra is another man's Mary Poppins."

As we reached each other, Tim waved. "Hi, Juli."

"Not exactly eloquent," I said as he went on.

Midge shrugged. "Well, a poet he's not. Juli, you're the belle of the ball, enjoy it. Don't be crying after someone who isn't available."

"You're right." But I turned around anyway and watched Tim striding down the hall.

* * *

After the lecture, Cliff drove up into the
hills and parked the car. He'd never done
that before and I nervously moved a little
nearer to the door. He noticed my furtive
maneuvers and said angrily, "I'm not going
to attack you, Juli."

I sighed as silently as I could. "I know
that, Cliff. I didn't think you were going
to."

He moved closer to me and put his
hand on my cheek, stroking it gently. I
saw the outline of his face in the pale
light of the moon. "You get more . . . I
don't know what . . . every day. Not just
prettier, though certainly that, but also
sweeter and smarter and everything. Juliet, let's go steady. We get along. We like
the same things, and I really like you a
lot."

I thought, *How did I get into this? How
can I get out of it?* I cleared my throat.
"Cliff, I like you a lot, too. But I don't want
to go steady with anyone. I'm not ready for
that. I just want to have fun and enjoy
being with you and —"

"Yeah. Me and Mike and Oliver and
anyone else who comes along."

Suddenly I felt tears running down my
face. "I seem to be hurting all my friends'
feelings lately. I don't mean to, but you're

angry and Mike was and Oliver was, and all I want is for all of us to be friends."

Cliff took me in his arms and kissed my cheek. "Don't cry, Juliet. Please. It's okay. I really understand. I guess I feel something you don't feel. You can't force it." His voice was soft and low. It was the kind of voice that could quote poetry on the phone.

He kissed my cheek again and started the car.

Before I went to sleep that night, I poured my heart and feelings and fears out into a new sonnet. The first line was, "If to grow up is to cause pain and sorrow . . ." Before I turned out the light I went to the window, looked out, and said aloud, "Romeo, all this is your fault." Then I turned my head in the direction of Timothy's house. "And yours, too, Timothy Thornton. If you knew I was alive, I wouldn't be giving out all these vibes to every passing boy."

Chapter Eleven

I wouldn't be going to college for another year and a half, but I was caught up in the big decision-making turmoil of where to go. I spent hours in the library, poring over catalogs, looking for the school that had the best program for me. I'd never seen a college or university that prepared a student for being a poet so I was anxious for the next best thing, a place with a good journalism program.

On an afternoon in early May, I was sitting at a table in the library surrounded by catalogs, when I felt someone sit down next to me. I looked up and stared into Timothy's green eyes. "Hi," he whispered.

No one else was in the library, but I whispered back, "Hi."

Tim motioned with his head to the pile of material at my elbow. "I think you have the University of Michigan catalog. Can I look at it?"

"Sure." I pushed it over to him. "Are you thinking of going there? It's a good school."

Timothy laughed in a peculiar way. "I don't think I'd ever get in. I'm not a brain, you know."

"That's not true, Tim. You're very smart. I'll bet if you worked hard you'd get in."

"No, Juliet. You're the brain, and your friends, Cliff and Oliver. Not me." He took the catalog and copied some information from it, while I watched his head bend closer to the paper he was writing on and his hand move swiftly across it. I wanted to reach out and touch that hand, just for a moment. Tim looked up and caught my eyes. He pushed the catalog back to me. "Thanks, Juli. See you around."

After he'd gone, I sat very still. It was the first time Timothy had ever said anything to me about his own feelings about himself. It had never occurred to me that there was anything about him he could be dissatisfied with. So Timothy Thornton was human after all. Not just a golden boy or a Prince Valiant, but a real person.

I was trying to assimilate this new thought when he came back to the table and sat down again. He was the Timothy I had always known — nice and low-key, but filled with assurance. "Listen, Jul, would you do me a favor?"

I couldn't imagine what I could do for Timothy Thornton, but I nodded my head.

"This may sound a little strange, but Deedee is having a bash Saturday night and Jim Morris's date got the measles, believe it or not."

Okay, I thought, *so Morris's date has the measles? What else is new?*

Tim looked embarrassed. "I was wondering if you'd go with him to the party. Everybody else already has a date and . . . oh, damn, that sounds terrible. I didn't mean —"

"It's okay, Tim. I know what you mean. But why doesn't Jim ask me himself? Wouldn't that make more sense?"

Tim pushed his hair back from his forehead. "Well, he said he had hardly ever spoken to you, and he thought you'd just say no."

"Why me, Tim? There are a lot of girls without dates."

"He said he thinks you're one of the greatest girls around."

And what do you think? I thought. It wasn't exactly reassuring to have your dream man trying to fix you up with a friend, but I was curious about how the other half of the world behaved at parties. Or, to be more honest, I wanted to spend an evening at the same party as Tim.

I fiddled with the papers on the table. "I'll go. If he calls and asks me himself."

"Great, Juli. Thanks. I'll tell him." He patted my shoulder and walked to the door.

I knew when the phone rang at eight that night that it would be Jim. I felt calm and not at all the way I once would have imagined I'd feel if one of the "beautiful people" at school was calling. But when he asked, "Is Juliet there?" I felt shock flood through me. The voice — something about the way he said Juliet — sounded familiar. Like Romeo? It wasn't anything I could easily define; nothing in the surface timbre of the voice, but underneath was a tone, a ring that reminded me of ... what?

After we had made all the arrangements about what time he'd pick me up, I walked slowly upstairs. The house was quiet. Barbara was studying with her door shut, Grandma was reading in her room, and Mother was in her room reading some papers she had brought home from the office. Often the stillness of the house, when I knew there were people in every room, made me feel safe and protected, as if I were engulfed in some cottony sleeping bag. But tonight I didn't want to be alone. I needed to talk to someone. I hesitated between Grandma's room and Mother's, not sure who I wanted. Then I walked into Grandma's. She looked up from the book she was reading and waited for me to say something. I sat on the edge of her bed and said, "That was Jim Morris on the phone. He's going to pick me up at eight on Saturday."

That wasn't at all what I wanted to say, but somehow I wasn't sure what I *did* want to talk about.

Grandma smiled. "You'll have a good time. I know it."

"I'm not sure. I won't know many people there — I mean know *well*. It's a crowd I've never been part of."

Grandma reached out and patted my knee. "You'll be the smartest and the prettiest girl there."

I laughed, stood up, and kissed the top of her head. She'd given me what I knew I'd come in for. Total love, total reassurance, total understanding. When I left her room I hesitated in front of Mother's door and went in, needing what I knew *she* had for me — reality.

Legal papers were scattered all over her bed, and she was sitting in an easy chair reading one of them. The room was big and cheerful with a brightly flowered bedspread and drapes. Highly polished light wood chests and a desk reflected the lights. I still found it hard to look at the king-size bed that dominated the room. I remembered so well my father sitting in bed reading, with his glasses on the edge of his nose. I looked away quickly, feeling tears come to my eyes.

"Are you busy?" I asked my mother.

"Yes, but if it's important I can stop for a little while."

I sat on the floor near her chair. "Jim

Morris invited me to a party Deedee Bennett is giving Saturday. I don't know if I really want to go. It just doesn't seem to be for *me*. And I don't know what the girls wear to this kind of thing." I pulled at a loose thread on the easy chair and looked above Mother's head.

She put down her papers and pushed my hand away from the thread. "Well, you can ask Deedee what to wear. That would solve *that* problem. And as for feeling nervous or concerned, that's natural. It's a new group for you. I feel that —"

She stopped and I looked at her. Her face had a slight pink flush, unlike her usual ivory paleness. "You feel what?" I asked.

"I feel nervous, too."

I laughed. "Because I'm going out with Jim Morris?"

She smiled. "No, because I have a . . . date . . . Saturday night, too."

I could actually feel my mouth drop open. "A *date?*" My mother had not gone out with anyone, even once, since my father had died.

She nodded her head. "Yes, a man who is a client of ours. He's divorced. He asked me to have dinner with him, and I said yes."

I felt alternating feelings of shock and anger and unreasonableness. She was entitled to go out. After all, Dad had been dead six years.

I cleared my throat. "That's nice, Mom. Really."

Mother peered at me. "You're lying, but I didn't expect you to like it."

I reached out for her hand. "Mom, I can't help how *I* feel, but I do understand how *you* feel." I didn't wait for her to say anything else. I just left.

I knocked on Barbara's door and went in when she called out, "Come in." Barbara was polishing her nails and was totally absorbed.

"Mother has a date for Saturday night," I said without any preliminaries.

Barbara looked up from her nails. "I know. She told me."

I felt anger and surprise. "How come she told you before she told me? I'm the oldest."

Barbara went back to her polishing, but said, "Maybe because she knew I'd be glad if she was glad, and you wouldn't be."

"That's a mean thing to say." I folded my arms and looked down at her with anger.

Barbara never raised her eyes. "It may be mean, but it's true. Isn't it?"

"Yes," I shouted at her and ran out of her room.

The next day I ran into Deedee in the women's room at school. "Jim Morris invited me to your party Saturday night."

Deedee smiled that smashing smile of hers. "Great. I'm glad you're coming."

I shrugged. "Well, he only asked me because his date has the measles."

Deedee reached out and patted the top of my head. "I don't think so. He's been looking at you from under those long brown lashes of his for weeks."

I leaned against the shelf under the mirror that ran halfway across the room. "Funny, I never noticed. Anyway, I don't know what to wear. I mean is it very informal or dressy, or what?"

Deedee was brushing her long blond hair until strands stood up with electricity. "Well, not *really* dressy but not old jeans either. A skirt with that frilly blouse we bought is just right."

I thanked her and started out of the room. Deedee called after me, "Hey, Jim is a nice guy. You'll like him."

I kept going through the door thinking, *If Tim is there I won't know poor Jim is alive.*

Saturday morning I weeded the lawn, feeling more and more anxious as the minutes passed. I didn't belong at that party. I wouldn't know what to say to anyone there. So I had some new clothes, and I had a Romeo calling, and my hair was longer, but I was still the same uncertain Juliet Gibson. I ached to call Jim Morris and tell him I had just been bitten by a tsetse fly and was about to succumb to a tropical disease.

As I debated whether I could, with any decency, break the date with Jim, Don, the postman, came up the walk holding a letter in his hand.

"Hi, Juli. A letter for you. It looks interesting."

I reached out for the letter, laughing inside at Don. He did everything but open the mail when he was curious. "Thanks, Don." He hung around for a few minutes, but when I put the envelope in my pocket he shrugged and walked away.

When he'd gone a few feet, I took the letter out of my pocket. I gasped as I saw who it was from. The *Orion Quarterly* was a literary magazine I had sent two poems to. I sat on the grass and tried to decide if I should ever open the envelope. As long as it was closed I could dream that I had sold a poem, but as soon as I opened it I'd know it was another rejection.

Finally, I tore the flap open slowly and pulled out the letter. I read two sentences and then rolled over and over on the grass, clutching the letter to me. *I had sold a poem!* I had sold a poem to the *Orion Quarterly.* I was a poet, a real, selling poet. Juliet Gibson, poet. Suddenly, the party that night was no longer frightening. I was Juliet Gibson, poet, and I was not going to feel uncertain with cheerleaders, or prom queens, or golden boys.

I ran into the house yelling, "Grandma! Mom! Barb! Anyone!"

Grandma came out of the kitchen, her hands full of flour. Mother came out of the bathroom, her hair dripping wet, and Barbara just called from upstairs, "What do you want?"

"I've sold a poem. I'm going to be a published poet, not just in the school magazine or the local paper, in a real magazine."

Grandma rushed over and grabbed me, kissing every part of my face she could reach. I looked up the stairs over Grandma's shoulder at Mother. She was smiling down at me, not saying anything, but her face was filled with such pride and respect

I could hardly pull my eyes away from her. Barbara appeared next to her in her short nightgown. "No kidding," she said, yawning. "What do you know?"

At dinner Saturday night, Barbara was in a robe with her hair in curlers. She was going to a party with Alf. I was wearing ragged blue jeans with my hair still wet from a vigorous shampoo, and Mother sat with us while she waited for her date to arrive. Grandma looked at her appraisingly. "You look lovely, Elizabeth." She sounded very pleased.

It never changes, I thought. Once you're a daughter, you're always part little girl to your mother. And once you're a mother, you always see your child in some ways that never alter. And does the boy/girl, man/woman relationship change as you get older? I watched my mother carefully. She was perched on the edge of her chair, obviously nervous, obviously unsure. Her blue eyes were wide and uneasy-looking. Her hands were tightly clenched in her lap, and she kept unclenching them and smoothing out the skirt of her suit.

She looked over at me and caught my stare. "I haven't gone out with a strange

man since before your father and I got engaged. That was a long time ago. I'm
scared."

"I know," I said softly. She looked re-
lieved.

Grandma said firmly, "You look lovely.
You *are* lovely. He's a lucky man."

Barbara, my mother, and I burst out
laughing at the same moment. "Mama,
you're treating me like Juliet or Barb,"
Mother said. "Do you know it?"

Grandma looked from Barbara to me to
Mother. "Yes, I know it, but that doesn't
stop what I said from being true."

Chapter Twelve

We all diplomatically disappeared before Mother's date arrived, so we wouldn't seem to be a committee that had assembled to pass on him. I peered out the window in Mother's bedroom as they left the house, but all I could see was the back of a man of about average height who had a bald spot on top of his head. As he opened the door for Mother and helped her into the car, I felt tears come to my eyes. *Daddy*, I cried inside.

I heard a sigh behind me and turned to see Barbara. She was paler than usual and her eyes were very wide as she watched Mother and her date. "I thought you felt this was a great idea," I said as I motioned to the parked car with my head.

"I do," she said shakily, "but it's scary, too."

She looked so little-girllike and lonely that I put my arms around her. For the briefest moment we clung to each other and then moved apart, embarrassed.

Not too long after Mother left, the doorbell rang. It was a little early for Jim, but I was ready and ran down the stairs. I felt good; all my earlier nervousness was gone. The Victorian blouse had been a good choice. The frills and high neck made me look almost from another century. My hair was now long enough to touch the top of the collar, and I liked the way it felt on my neck.

I pulled open the door. Oliver stood there, shuffling from one foot to another. When he saw how I was dressed, he stopped shuffling. "I was going to ask you if you wanted to go to a movie, but I think I'm too late."

"I'm sorry, Oliver, but I have a . . . date. Do you want to come in for a few minutes anyway?"

Oliver backed away. "Hell, no. Who is it? Cliff? Mike?"

"No." I paused for a moment, not sure I

wanted to tell him who I was going out with. But this was Oliver, my dear old friend. How could I not? "It's Jim Morris."

"Morris! The big time, eh? Well, I guess I have to start asking a few weeks in advance."

"Oliver. That's crazy."

He leaned over and kissed my cheek. "Not so crazy." Then he walked away.

"Oliver. Wait! I have to tell you! I sold a poem to the *Orion Quarterly*." I held my breath waiting to see if he was just going to keep walking away from me. But he turned and ran back. He put his arms around me and lifted me off the ground. "Juli, that's — that's great. Which poem?"

" 'Uncertainty.' "

Oliver hugged me again. "I'd better go before Morris arrives. I'll come over tomorrow afternoon and buy you an ice cream cone to celebrate."

By the time Jim rang the bell about fifteen minutes later, I felt exhausted. Between Mother's date and the excitement over the poem, I had expended just about as much emotion as I wanted to that night, and I still had the party to get through.

"Hi, Juli," he said, sounding very strange.

"Come on in."

He walked into the living room and sat down immediately. I looked at him closely. He was just as good-looking as he'd ever been, but his nose was red, his cheeks were flushed, and there was a slight film of perspiration on his forehead.

"Jim, you look sick," I said with concern.

"It's nothing," he said hoarsely. "Just a slight cold."

Grandma came into the room energetically, ready to look my date over. I wondered what she would do if she didn't like him. Lock me in a closet? Order him from the house?

She took one look at Jim and said, "You're sick." She went over to him and put her hand on his forehead. "You have a fever, too."

He sank back into the chair, then pulled himself forward. "It's nothing. Just a slight cold," he repeated. He stood up and took my arm firmly. "Come on, Juli. We'll be late."

Grandma started protesting, but Jim had steered me out of the door and to his car before she could say anything more. The drive to Deedee's took just five minutes, but it was long enough to have all the morning's anxieties swoop down on me again. *How did I get into this?*

As we walked up the steps to Deedee's front door, my heart was pounding and I could feel a trickle of perspiration slide down my arm. So much for the anti-perspirants that are supposed to keep you dry in *any* emergency. Then a voice in my head said, *You're Juliet Gibson, poet. About to be published in the* Orion Quarterly. A smaller voice said, *Yes, and you've got a Romeo, too.* I straightened up, feeling almost confident.

Deedee opened the door for us. "Glad you're here," she said. "Everyone is down-stairs. You two go on down. I just want to stir the chili."

The Bennetts had a finished basement and it was crowded with kids, mostly the stars of school. Football players and ac-tresses and cheerleaders and prom queens and track stars — and just plain gorgeous people like Tim. Some kids were dancing and some were hanging around talking and a few couples were cuddled up in the big easy chairs in the room. Several of them waved to me absentmindedly but they didn't seem unfriendly. I knew most of them, but really only from afar.

Tim was putting some records on the

stereo when he saw us. He left it and walked over. "Hi, Jul. Jim."

"Hi," Jim mumbled weakly. "Want to dance, Juli?"

"Sure." I turned to Tim regretfully. "Talk to you later?"

A slow tune was playing, and Jim took me into his arms. He put his cheek against mine and I could feel the heat rising from it. *One hundred and one degrees at least*, I thought. He sniffled and coughed as we moved slowly around the room, and I could hardly keep from laughing. My big night with the other half of the world, and my date was sniffling in my ear as we danced.

"Hey, Juli, I hope you don't catch this from me."

I patted his shoulder. "Don't worry, Jim. I'll be fine."

He shook his head sadly. "I've really been looking forward to this, and here I am half-dead. I'm sorry."

I moved my head from his cheek and looked at him. "Why were you?"

Jim was baffled. "Why was I what?"

"Why were you looking forward to dating me?"

Jim was now not only baffled but at a loss for words. "What kind of question is that to ask? I was looking forward to this because . . . you're cute."

I put my cheek back next to his and thought about that. I had never in all my sixteen years thought of myself as cute. I knew very well I was not the cute type. I was too tall, too thin, too direct. Cute to me was Midge, small and cuddly and adorable-looking. I guessed cuteness was in the eye of the beholder.

"I sold a poem to the *Orion Quarterly*," I said suddenly.

"Where's Orion? Around here somewhere?" Jim asked between sneezes.

"It's a literary magazine," I answered.

"Oh," he said.

The music stopped and Tim was standing next to us. "Dance, Juli?"

It was his duty dance of the evening, but I was going to enjoy it. He held me lightly in his arms and I wished he would hold me tighter, the way Jim had, but he didn't. "Thanks for coming, Juli. You look great."

As he talked he didn't look down at me, but across the room where Jim was talking to Deedee. I wanted him to be aware of me, to remember he was holding me, so I swayed slightly and came down heavily on his foot. He jumped and I smiled. "Sorry," I said. I wasn't sure why, but I felt better.

I watched the "stars" carefully that night, while I danced and ate chili and drank Cokes and talked to a few of the kids. I didn't know what I had expected, but the stars weren't doing anything different than the nonstars did at parties. They weren't sneaking drinks or smoking pot or making out or even showing off. In reality it was a dull party. I drifted from group to group, listening to the conversations about the various games of the year, the parties everyone had been to, the latest gossip, school talk. I waited to hear someone talk about no more nukes, or polluting the environment, or the latest John Irving book, or something like that, but it wasn't part of their world. It didn't make them unlikable, just not very interesting.

I was shocked and somewhat disoriented by that fact, and I kept thinking that since Tim had danced his one dance with me I'd just as soon be home.

At about midnight, I decided it was a respectable hour to go home, and realized I hadn't seen Jim for a long time. I looked around the room and saw him fast asleep in an armchair. His mouth was open slightly, dragging in the air his poor, stuffed nose couldn't accommodate. As I walked over to him, Tim came up to me. "What a crummy thing for him to do."

I shook my head. "He's sick, Tim. He really shouldn't have come. I'll have to get him home."

Tim put his arm around my shoulders lightly. "I'll drive you both," he said. I felt the warmth of his fingers on my shoulder, and turned to look at him. But at that moment he bent over Jim, shaking him slightly. "Wake up, Jim. I'm going to take you home."

Jim just huddled deeper into the chair. Deedee came over, looking concerned. "What's the matter with him?"

"He must have the flu," I answered.

Tim pulled Jim out of his chair and said to Deedee, "I'm going to drive him and Juli home. I'll be back soon."

Deedee put her hand on my arm and asked, "Did you have a good time, Juli?"

I was touched by the warmth in her eyes, surprised she wasn't just assuming that if you were at a star's party you had a good time. "Sure, Deedee. It was great."

Tim and I half-carried, half-pulled a very out-of-it Jim into the car. He fell into the backseat and was asleep again immediately.

As Tim turned the key in the ignition, he said, "I'll drop him off first. I may need your help getting him inside. Then I'll take you home."

When we got to Jim's house, we lugged him up to his door, found his key in his pocket, and got him inside. His father came into the hall and asked with a perceivable amount of terror in his voice, "Is he drunk?"

"He's sick, Mr. Morris," Tim answered. "I think he has the flu."

"What a relief," Jim's father said.

When Tim and I were back in the car, we both started to laugh. "It's okay, Mr. Morris, he's not drunk, he only has leprosy," I said between laughs.

Tim started the car, still laughing. I realized it was the first time I had ever been alone with him. Suddenly I was aware of his soft breathing, and the way he hunched slightly over the steering wheel, and his leg not touching mine. I was filled with a yearning I could hardly bear.

We got to my house and Tim turned to me. "Sorry about Jim."

"It's okay." Some of the yearning I was feeling must have shown, because Tim leaned over and brushed my cheek with his lips.

"Night. Thanks for coming."

I nodded my head and turned away quickly, not wanting him to see the tears in my eyes, opened the car door, and ran up the path to my house.

As I walked upstairs, I heard the radio on in my mother's room, so I knocked softly on the door. "Come on in," she called.

I watched her brushing her hair as I stood in the door. Without any makeup, the smudges under her eyes were more apparent, but she was still lovely-looking.

"Have a good time?" I asked. "I hope you did," I said earnestly.

She motioned to me to come in and I sat on the edge of her bed. "It was okay. Strange. I wasn't sure what to talk about all the time. But, you know what? He wasn't sure what to talk about either. He's newly divorced. So we were both in the same boat."

"Are you going to see him again?"

Mother stopped brushing and looked at me. "I think so. He was nice. What about you? Have a good time?"

"It was okay." I started toward her door and turned back to her. I don't think I'll ever know why I told her, but I did. I just wanted to feel close to someone.

"Mother, there is a boy — man — who

calls and recites love poetry from *Romeo and Juliet* to me and then hangs up."

She looked down at the brush in her hands and pulled a brown hair from it, examining it with interest. Then she looked up. "I know. Grandma told me." She waited for me to say something, but I was trying to sort out how I felt.

Mother said quickly, "She wasn't divulging a confidence. She was worried and thought I should know. Don't be angry at her, Juliet, or at me."

"I'm not, really. Anyway, I know he's a nice person. Romeo, I mean."

Mother looked confused and upset. "He probably is, but I must admit I wish he weren't calling. It makes me feel creepy. What does he say?"

I smiled and then tried to look very casual. "Things like, 'It is my lady; O, it is my love,' and 'Did my heart love till now?' and 'Why art thou yet so fair?' "

Mother stared at me with wide eyes. "Heavens. My little Juliet, getting literary, romantic calls."

"It's been nice, Mother."

She went back to her brushing. "Well, they did get you out of the baggy pants, so that's something. But I wish he'd stop."

I leaned over and kissed her. "Don't worry. Good night."

In my room I sat on the floor, in my favorite position, and rested my chin on the windowsill. I thought about Tim and Romeo and a Millay sonnet I loved. The last line was, "Once more I clasp, and there is nothing there."

Could it be Tim? I wondered suddenly. Could Tim be Romeo?

Then I laughed out loud at my wishful thinking. Impossible. Tim was practically glued to Deedee. Anyway, I knew he could never disguise his voice so I wouldn't recognize it. I had repeated almost every word to myself that he had ever said. I knew his voice as well as Midge's. And Tim was the last boy in the world to quote Shakespeare. It just wasn't his thing.

Chapter Thirteen

The first thing I thought of when I woke up the next morning was not the party, or Jim, or Tim, or Romeo, but that Grandma had told my mother about the calls. I always trusted Grandma totally, and she had never, that I knew of, done anything to shake that trust. Yet, now she had. I remembered saying to her, *"I don't want anyone else to know."* Why had she told Mother? I felt a terrible empty space in me where the total trust had been and wondered if I could ever fill it.

Then I heard *her* voice: *"Grandmas are one thing, mothers are another. Mothers are the ones who should have the troubles."*

You know how sometimes adults are so mystifying and other times they are so transparent, and how they can become understandable in one clarifying moment? Well, suddenly I understood.

Grandma wanted to be a grandma to me. She was willing and wanted to be a mother to *her* daughter, but she wanted *me* to be a granddaughter. I knew there was a difference, subtle but real. I didn't understand all the elements in the difference, but part of it was the responsibility and the involvement and the worry. I was beginning to unscramble my own feelings about the two of them — what I wanted from them, and what I could expect from them. I had always loved Grandma unequivocably. Now I was also filled with a deep compassion and love for Mother, with the blue smudges under her eyes, and the shortness in her voice at times, and her date, and her expecting me and Barbara to shape up.

When I went into the kitchen everyone was eating breakfast, and everyone was eating something different. I poured a glass of juice and patted my mother's shoulder as I went by her chair.

She looked up with surprise. "What was that for?"

I shrugged. "Just felt like it."

At that moment the phone rang. Mother got up, saying, "I'll get it. It's probably my boss. She's going out of town for a few days and said she'd call this morning with a few last-minute messages."

Mother picked up the phone. "Hello." She paused as she listened to the voice at the other end, and then her pale skin flushed slightly. She turned away from us and said in a low voice, "Well, thank you, Walt, I had a good time, too. . . . Yes, sure. I'd like that. . . . Fine. . . . Bye."

Barbara and I exchanged sly glances. "Is Walt your date?" I asked.

Mother busily added sugar to her coffee. "Yes, he is."

I looked at Barbara and said, "I don't know. *My* date fell fast asleep last night, and he isn't calling *me* this morning."

Barbara took it from there. "And Alfie spent the whole night playing one of those dumb video games on Joyce's TV set, and he isn't calling *me* this morning."

I buttered some toast and bit off a piece. "Maybe Mother will tell us some of her dating secrets, so we get that kind of consideration."

"Girls," Grandma said firmly, "leave your mother alone."

Mother stirred her coffee. "Well, you know, I don't think I'm going to tell either of you anything. You'll have to learn it by yourselves. Just call me a femme fatale."

She got up and left the kitchen, swinging her hips. We laughed at her, but I know that I felt happy for her pleasure, yet put off by it.

When I looked at Grandma, she was watching me carefully. "Your father has been dead for six years. It's time your mother started seeing other men if she wants to. Living in the past isn't much fun."

"I know," I said. "It's just hard to get used to."

"Life is filled with getting used to all sorts of things," Grandma said. "Some good, some bad, and some in the middle."

"Isn't it early for a lecture?" Barbara asked.

Grandma looked at Barbara and shook her head. "How do fourteen-year-old girls turn into smart-alecks so fast?" But she leaned over and kissed Barbara's cheek.

When I went upstairs, Mother's door was open. She was making the big bed so I got on one side and helped straighten the blankets. "Tell me about your party," she said.

127

I pulled a blanket tight. "It was just so-so. The kids were nice, but not very interesting. I thought it was going to be a really exciting night, but it was just a night. Then Jim was sick and fell asleep."

"How did you get home?" Mother asked.

"Tim drove us." I didn't meet her eyes, but I felt her looking at me. "Okay, so I like him. But what's the use? He doesn't know I'm alive. I'm little, or not-so-little Juliet Gibson, whom he's known all his life. I'm part of the scenery, like the statue of John Dell downtown." I sat on the freshly made bed.

"Juli, we just made the bed. Get up."

I ignored her and went on complaining. "You're the mother. Mothers on TV are so wise. So say something wise. You want me to talk to you, well, I'm talking. Now talk back."

Mother sat down next to me. "The hell with the bed," she said. "Juli, I'm not so wise, but I do know this. You're smart and talented and beautiful. Don't waste your time longing for a boy who doesn't know you're alive. There's no sense to it, and it can't be much fun."

I stood up and brushed the wrinkles off the bedspread. "Well, what you said is wise, but not very helpful, since if a person is longing, she's longing. I mean I can't turn it off like a bad TV program."

Mother said sadly, "I know. I'm the last one to give advice like that. Well, maybe someone else will come along and distract you — like your Romeo."

"He's a big help," I said angrily. "He's just a voice on the telephone."

That afternoon Oliver came over, just as he'd said he would. "Come on, get your bike and we'll go downtown. I promised you an ice cream cone and I'm not the kind of guy who goes back on his word."

As we biked along at a good brisk pace, he yelled against the wind, "How does it feel to be published in the *Orion Quarterly*? That's the big time."

"It feels great," I yelled back. "But how do I follow my own act?"

"You get more things published. You plan ahead. You set goals," he answered.

We had reached the ice cream parlor and parked our bikes. "You make it sound so easy," I said.

He put his arm around my waist as we walked into the store. "Who said it was easy? What do you want?" he asked. "The sky's the limit. Two scoops? Three? long as it isn't a banana split."

We both ordered double-scoop cones and went to the back where there were little tables and chairs. We sat down and slurped away happily, trying each other's cones, comparing tastes, and seriously debating the joys of chocolate versus strawberry. In the same casual tone he had used while defending his passion for strawberry ice cream, he said, "Will you go to the Spring Dance with me? I'm probably not asking early enough. It's only two weeks away."

I stopped licking the cone and let the ice cream drip down over my fingers. "I've never been to the Spring Dance."

"Neither have I," Oliver said. "I don't imagine it offers much competition to the Inaugural Ball, but if you think the Dellwood Inn is an ideal place to spend a Saturday night you'll love it."

I wiped the ice cream off my fingers and smiled happily at Oliver. "I'd really like to go with you. It sounds great."

"You have no taste," Oliver said, smiling equally happily.

Then he became serious. "Juliet, you remember the day we had dinner with you, when we first got back to Dellwood?"

"Sure," I answered.

"You showed me a poem you'd written and when I asked who it was about you said, 'Someone who doesn't know I'm alive.' What I'm curious about is who's the guy?"

I looked away from him for a minute and then said, "Really, Oliver, it's nothing. I mean, just a fantasy kind of thing. You know."

I didn't like lying to Oliver, but there was truth in what I had said. Timothy Thornton was just a fantasy, as far as our ever having any real relationship.

Oliver grinned. "Then there's hope for me. Right?"

I grinned back. "Right."

When I got home, Mother told me, "Midge called. Deedee called. And Mike called. But Mike said he was going out and would call you back."

I ran upstairs, pulled the phone into my room, and called Midge. I had spoken to her that morning and given her a blow-by-blow description of the party, so I knew her call wasn't about that. "What's up?" I asked when she answered her phone.

"Nothing. I'm bored and thought I'd come over, if you're not busy."

I moved across the room, untwisting the curled phone cord. "Sure, come on. I'm not doing anything."

131

Then I called Deedee. "Hi. Mom said you called."

Deedee said considerately, "I hope you had a good time last night. I mean, what with Jim falling asleep and everything, it couldn't have been one of your favorite parties."

"It was fine, Deedee. Actually, Jim's conking out gave me more of a chance to talk to a lot of people. It was a great party." I hoped she believed me.

Deedee breathed a sigh of relief. "I'm awfully glad you liked it. Listen, feel like coming over for a while?"

I paused, unsure, then said before I could change my mind, "Midge is coming over here, so if we could both walk over to your house, it would be fine."

"The more the merrier," Deedee said.

As Midge and I walked over to Deedee's house a little later, Midge asked, "Does Deedee's room look like Deedee?"

I shrugged. "I don't know. I never got upstairs. But I'm sure it's all pink and white with a fancy dressing table and everything neat and in place."

Midge agreed. "It probably smells of perfume, and I'll bet she has Renoir prints on the walls."

We laughed and I didn't feel guilty kidding about Deedee because we were both doing it without any malice. When we got to Deedee's, she said, "Come on up to my room. It's the only place we'll have any privacy."

The door to her room was shut and as she pushed it open, Deedee said, "It's a little messy."

Midge and I exchanged glances and smiled. When we walked into Deedee's room we both stood still, trying to take it all in. I had seen messy rooms before, but Deedee's boggled the mind. There was not one place on the bed, bureau, bookcase top, and desk that wasn't cluttered with clothes, jewelry, books, socks, magazines, and dirty dishes. Deedee smiled shyly. "I'm not much for neatness, as you can see." She pushed everything to the back of the bed and motioned to us to sit down. Midge and I could not look at each other.

Midge got up and crossed the room to a big bulletin board over Deedee's desk. On it were tacked pictures of about ten different buildings.

Midge looked at them closely. "You have a thing for buildings?" she asked.

Deedee smiled. "I'm going to be an architect. Those buildings are the ones I think are the most beautiful in the world."

I couldn't believe how mistaken I'd been about Deedee, thinking she was shallow and not serious.

We talked about our plans for the future. I told her about selling my poem, and Midge talked about wanting her own catering business some day. We laughed a lot. I told Deedee what Midge and I had thought her room would look like and we laughed some more.

Then I remembered. "Hey. Oliver invited me to the Spring Dance."

Midge said with surprise, "How come you waited this long to tell me?"

"Well, on the way over here we were so busy decorating Deedee's room I didn't have time."

Deedee looked pleased. "I'm going with Tim. Maybe we can all go together."

Out of the corner of my eye, I could see Midge watching me. "I don't know. I'd have to talk to Oliver about it."

Midge glanced at Deedee and then looked away. "That must make you happy — going with Tim, I mean."

A strange, fleeting look crossed Deedee's face. "Tim is sweet and nice and I like him a lot, but, well, he's not Henry Winberg."

I couldn't believe what she was saying. "You like *Henry Winberg?*"

Deedee smiled. "Yes, but he never even *looks* at me."

"That's because he never comes out of the chem lab," Midge said.

It was very hard to put together. I loved Tim, and Tim loved Deedee, and Deedee loved Henry Winberg, and Henry loved the chem lab. I tried to digest all this and then heard Midge's impatient voice. "Juliet! Have you thought about what you're going to wear to the dance? Jeans won't do."

I came back to reality quickly. "Heavens, no. I can't ask Mom for another penny for clothes, and I have the grand total of ten dollars saved. That won't go far."

"What about the money you're going to get for selling your poem?" Midge asked.

"It's not much," I answered slowly. "Anyway, I don't want to spend that money on a dress. I want to use it for things I can keep forever, so I'll always be able to look at them and remember my first real sale."

Deedee was interested. "What do you think you'll spend the money on?"

I leaned against a pile of debris on Deedee's bed. "Some poetry books, records, maybe a new wristwatch — stuff like that."

We were all silent for a few minutes. Then Deedee said, "Maybe someone could make something for you. Does your mother sew?"

I laughed. "My mother can barely thread a needle, much less sew."

Deedee tried again. "How about your grandmother?"

I shook my head. "She knits like a dream, but she can't sew, either. So unless I want to go with an afghan wrapped around me, she's out, too."

Suddenly Deedee went to her closet. As she opened it, a tennis racquet, an old stuffed animal, and a box of shoes fell out. She pulled out a long dress and held it up. "Listen, my grandmother sent this to me last Christmas. Look at it. It's just not me, but Juli, if you wanted — I mean, it would be perfect for you. You could borrow it, easy."

I could see it wasn't right for Deedee, who was the most contemporary-looking girl I knew. It reminded me of the blouse she had picked out for me. The dress was pale lilac with a high ruffled neck and long sleeves with a ruffle around each cuff. It fell in soft folds and there were two bands of ruffles around the bottom of the dress. The belt was made of a deep purple ribbon that cascaded to the hem of the dress.

Deedee held it up to me and pushed me to her mirror. "It's beautiful," she whispered. "Please wear it."

"What about your grandmother?" I asked. "Won't she be angry?"

"She'll never know, and if she finds out maybe it will make her realize I'm not the Victorian-girl type."

I pressed the dress against me. "I never thought of *myself* that way either."

"You're a little bit of a lot of things," Deedee said. She turned to Midge. "Tell her to wear it, Midge."

Midge knew better than to try to push me into taking the dress, but she did say, "It looks good."

"Okay," I said suddenly, "I'll wear it." I turned to Deedee. "You're really so nice. Thanks."

She took the dress and folded it carefully, putting it into a paper bag she somehow found in the closet. "Take it with you now. It needs to be pressed and stuff."

That night I called Jim to see if he was still alive. I spoke to his father who said, "Jim wants to talk to you. Wait."

After a few minutes, a gravelly voice said, "Juliet, I would have called you today, but I've been feeling so crummy. I'm sorry about last night. Really."

"It's okay, Jim. How do you feel?"

Jim cleared his throat. "Pretty awful, but listen, I want to ask you, will you go to the Spring Dance with me? I know it's sort of late to ask, but —"

"Your date has the mumps," I joked.

Jim laughed with embarrassment. "I have no date, Juli. I mean, you're the first girl I've asked. I want to go with *you*."

I was surprised and I have to admit, pleased that this time I wasn't just second choice to a communicable disease. "I'm sorry, Jim, but I'm going with Oliver."

"Damn," Jim said softly. "I knew I waited too long."

"Only a few hours too long. Oliver just asked me this afternoon. I'm not usually dated up weeks in advance."

"Good," Jim answered. "Look, when I get back to school, we'll make another date. Right now I don't think I'm going to live."

"Want to bet?" I laughed. "Go back to bed, Jim, drink lots of liquids, watch rotten TV programs, and sleep. You'll live, I know it."

His voice sounded more normal when he said, "Juliet, you're really great."

The voice — was there something in the voice? But then I thought, *Ridiculous. Never Jim.*

Chatper Fourteen

The next day was Grandma's birthday. She had spent all afternoon in New York with friends, having lunch, going to the theater, shopping, things Grandma loved to do.

Mother came home from work early, and she and Barbara and I fixed a special birthday dinner. Mother was a terrible cook, but she was a wild, fancy cake-maker. The more gunk she could pile on it the happier she was. So Barb and I took care of baking a chicken and cleaning fresh asparagus and whipping potatoes, while Mother carefully spelled out Happy Birthday in pink on a chocolate cake. Since there was already a whole bottle of maraschino cherries on the cake, it wasn't easy to fit the writing on, too.

Barbara watched silently. Then she said, "It's good you have brains and beauty, because you aren't going to get to any man's heart through his stomach. Provided, of course, you want to get to any man's heart."

We waited for Mom to answer, but she ignored us and started trying to put candles between the cherries. When the phone rang, I answered it with a cheerful hello.

And there was the voice:

"The brightness of her cheek
    would shame those stars,
As daylight does a lamp."

I was silent for so long that Mother and Barbara looked at me. They knew by the expression on my face who was on the phone. You know how people say that at some moments your life flashes before you? Well, mine did then. I saw Mother struggling to keep up our house; Grandma, running the place without complaints; and Barbara, trying to grow up. I thought of my poem in the *Orion Quarterly*, my hair curling on my neck, and Midge, and the friendships I had had for years with Cliff, Oliver, and Mike.

"Don't," I said to the caller. "Don't call

me anymore! You're not fair, and I don't like it. So just stop calling."

Barbara stared at me wide-eyed. Her mouth pursed into an *ooh*. Mother licked some icing off a finger with an expression I couldn't figure out.

The caller was silent. I couldn't even hear him breathing. Then he said softly, "Good-bye, Juliet." I knew the voice. I knew it and I stretched my memory as far as I could to place it, but recognition eluded me.

As I hung up the phone, Barbara said, "Wow. I don't believe it!"

Mother just said, "I'm glad!"

I went up to my room right after the call and sat down by the window. The sky was a bright blue with little puffy clouds. The sun was soft and hazy, having lost its daytime power. I tried to figure out why I had told Romeo not to call. I hadn't *ever* thought of doing it. I'd gotten angry at him, but I had never wanted him to go away. Now he certainly wouldn't call again, and I'd never have the wonderful feeling of being a part of a drama unfolding in an otherwise ordinary life. I'd never find out who he was, and what he thought was so wonderful about me.

I tested myself. If I had it to do all over

again, right now, would I tell him not to call? I knew I would, even though it didn't make me happy. I had always thought that when you were confronted with two choices, one would make you happy and one wouldn't. One was right and one was wrong. Now I realized that sometimes you had two choices, neither one of which would make you happy. One just seemed better than the other, but neither one was great.

I knew I didn't need Romeo's calls the way I had in the beginning; that I had to be free to find a real Romeo if that was what I wanted to do; and that I couldn't settle for an unknown voice on the phone. I felt more grown-up, but feeling grown-up wasn't totally wonderful either, much to my surprise. Life was a lot more complicated than I had thought it was.

That night after dinner, Midge came over with a bottle of cologne for Grandma. Grandma was grandma to most of my friends, especially the ones who didn't have grandmas of their own. She opened the present and immediately splashed some of the cologne on her neck, kissing Midge and leaning over so Midge could smell the sweet scent.

We all sat in the big living room, something we didn't do much anymore, and admired Grandma's presents. I felt lonely and proud at the same time. I knew I would miss Romeo's calls, and yet I knew I had had to tell him to stop.

Barbara said what all of us were thinking, "Who do you suppose it was?"

Midge answered immediately, "I think it was Mike."

"Why?" I asked. "I mean, I think it might be, but I'm not sure."

Midge sounded confident. "It's Mike, because he's least likely to do something like that. He'd feel it was safe to call and quote from *Romeo and Juliet*, because no one would think a jock would do that."

I remembered the softness of his voice the day he said, "I think I'm in love with you." It could be Mike.

Barbara interrupted my thoughts. "You're wrong, Midge. It's Cliff."

Midge shook her head. "Why Cliff? How can you sound so sure?"

"Well, I never mentioned it, because — well, just because. But one day when I came home Juli said she'd had a call and that was the day I had seen Cliff in a phone booth downtown."

"Honestly, Barb, just because Cliff was

in a phone booth doesn't mean he's Romeo. I mean, anyone can go into a phone booth." I looked at her condescendingly.

"How many times do you use a booth in town?" she asked smugly.

"Not often," I admitted. "But I do sometimes. I called Midge from a booth not too long ago."

But I remembered Cliff's voice and touch when he had parked his car in the hills. It could be Cliff.

Mother got up out of her chair and leaned against the fireplace, facing us. "This is ridiculous, trying to figure out who the caller is. But it can only be Oliver. Oliver is the likely one to do something as literate as quote poetry. You know that, Juli."

I shrugged, but secretly I thought, *Yes, Oliver is the most likely to do something like that.*

Grandma laughed. "You're *all* wrong. How can you be so dense? Of course, it's that Jim with the flu. It isn't someone Juliet has known for years. It's someone new. It's Jim. As soon as I saw him sniffing and coughing that night he called for you, I knew."

I went over and put my arms around Grandma. "Grandma, how can you say that? Jim was the least romantic figure in the world that night."

She agreed. "That's why. Any boy who could be as sick as he was and *still* take you to that party has to be crazy about you. Crazy enough to go out sick and crazy enough to make phone calls like Romeo's."

I remembered the night Jim had called to invite me to Deedee's party, the way I had reacted to his voice saying "Juliet." It had struck some chord of response in me. It could be Jim.

Or Tim? I thought. Then, *What a hopeless fool you are!*

I started walking up and down the room restlessly. "I don't know. Midge, maybe it's Davey Feiner. Remember, we talked about that once?"

Midge looked a little embarrassed. "I don't think so. He asked me to the Spring Dance today. He said he'd been wanting to ask me out for months, but he was just too shy to do it."

I was happy. "Great! Let's go together. You and Davey and me and Oliver."

Midge looked unsure. "I don't know. He worked up the courage to talk to me, but I'm not sure he's got the strength to include you and Oliver in that. He may be totally silent all night."

146

I laughed. "That's okay. Oliver talks enough for two people anyway. Well, this whole discussion hasn't helped at all. I still don't know who the caller is."

Mother agreed. "Besides, it could be someone who has never said a word to you, except over the phone. It could be anyone at all. Someone who has just loved you from afar," she added dramatically.

That night when I was in bed, I thought about the phrase Mother had used jokingly, "*Someone who has just loved you from afar.*" It had appealed to me when she said it. It had brought to mind all the great lovers of history, but now as I cuddled under the blankets I thought about what I wanted for myself. I had been spending a lot of time thinking about who Romeo was, and what I was going to wear to the dance, and whether Tim was aware of me, and it upset me. My life felt out of whack. It wasn't familiar to me anymore. And more important, I felt frightened. I got out of bed and went into the hall. I hesitated, looking at Mother's closed door and Grandma's. I wanted to be held and cuddled and babied. I moved toward Grandma's door and then stopped. A voice inside my head said, *Mother.* But I didn't open her door, either.

I went back to my room and turned on the light. I opened my closet and started rummaging through it, pushing things around on the floor. Then I climbed up on a chair and looked on the shelf and found what I had been searching for. I pulled out Boris, an old stuffed turtle. He was worn and faded. He had been cried on, and cuddled, and thrown across the room, and stuffed into overnight bags, and had survived.

I got back into bed and held him close to me. I used to talk to him when I was a kid and it always helped. Boris had seen me through almost-failed tests, fights with Barb, parties I hadn't been invited to, and even my father's death.

At first I felt awkward and embarrassed. "Hey, Boris. Remember me? Little Juli, who is big Juli now?"

As I spoke, I relaxed, and my low voice became less shaky. "Boris, I'm not very happy. I'm confused and upset. Look at me, I have more boys than I know what to do with, and you know, they seem to be getting in the way of my life. But are they really? I'm still writing my poetry. I'm still doing well in school. I'm not seeing any less of Midge. And I've even found a new friend, Deedee. I feel closer to Mother than ever, and I'm more human to Barb. So what's bothering me?

"What's bothering me is that I don't want a *lot* of boyfriends. I want a lot of boys who are *friends* and I want one *boyfriend*, for now. Maybe next year I'll want something different, but right now I just want to know how it feels to have something nice and special with *one* boy.

"Maybe it's easier being a turtle. I mean, do girl turtles have as much trouble as girl girls?"

I cradled Boris in my arms. Moonlight was falling on the framed letter from the *Orion Quarterly*. I got up and took Boris over to it. I held him up. "See. Bet you didn't think *that* would ever happen. Bet you didn't think I'd still be mooning over Timothy Thornton all these years, either. You would have done better with a different owner; a girl who was *really* sensible, not one who just gets to the dentist on time."

I got back into bed and, holding Boris tight, fell asleep. When I woke up in the morning, Barb was shaking my shoulder. "You're late. You forgot to set your alarm."

I tried to hide Boris under the covers, but Barb just smiled. "It's okay. I still go

149

to bed with my old crib blanket sometimes. And you should see what *that* looks like."

When I walked into the cafeteria at lunch time, I looked for the boys and Midge at our table. As I went over to them, Deedee yelled from her table, "Hey, Juliet. Here."

I looked over at her. Tim was sitting next to her, Jim was there, and about four more of the beautiful people. Once I would have felt flattered to be wanted by them. I liked Deedee, I liked Jim, I loved Tim, but I wanted to be with my close friends. I waved to Deedee and called, "Can't. See you later."

Cliff and Oliver pulled an extra chair to the table for me. Cliff was reading a book about Freud; Mike was diagramming some basketball plays on a paper napkin; Oliver was doing a math assignment; Midge was trying to figure out what the dessert they called rice pudding really was.

A few tables away, I saw Davey Feiner staring at Midge. I motioned to him to join us, but he just turned red and shook his head. Midge tore herself away from the rice pudding and said, "I tried to get him to come over before, but he isn't about to. I don't think he's even going to be able to say hello to my mother and father when he picks me up next week."

"What's next week?" Cliff asked.

Midge tasted the rice pudding again and looked more puzzled than before. "Spring Dance. Davey and I are going, and if I can manage it, we're going to double with Oliver and Juliet."

Mike and Cliff both stared at me. "You're going to the dance with Oliver?" Mike asked.

"Yes," I answered, starting to feel guilty.

"How come?" Cliff asked tightly.

"How come? Because I asked her," Oliver said just as tightly.

I watched the three boys closely, watched their eyes narrow, their hands clench, and their breathing become a little faster.

"Here we go again," Midge said.

"No, we are *not* going again," I said firmly. "Stop it. Just stop it. You know what? You don't really feel angry at each other because of me. You're all just competitive, in general. If it weren't me you were competing for, it would be something else. So stop it. I'm not something you bounce back and forth. I don't like it."

I was shouting. People were looking at

me and there was silence at the tables around us. We were the most interesting thing that had happened in the cafeteria since — by some mistake — there was a good lunch served a year ago.

The boys looked at me with astonishment. I was not a scene-maker usually. "Come on, Juli," Cliff said, "Calm down."

"No, I won't. Not until you three start acting like human beings. We're friends, all of us. If a little jewelry, and a little perfume, and some jeans that fit start this kind of misery, then who needs it?" I took off the earrings and the bracelets I was wearing. I dumped water on some napkins and scrubbed my neck where I had sprayed perfume. And I knotted my jacket around my waist, covering the tight jeans.

"Take it off," someone yelled across the room.

"Shut up," Oliver yelled back. "Juli, come on. We didn't mean to upset you. Honest."

"Well, you *have* upset me. And I meant what I said on the phone. Whichever one of you is calling, stop that, too."

The boys all looked at me and I tried to see which one looked guilty, but they *all* did.

"Look at me," I shouted. "I'm still Juliet

Gibson. Still the same girl. So my hair is longer and I dress a little better and I sell poems, but I'm still Juli. What's with you guys?"

Suddenly Tim and Deedee were at the table. "You okay, Juli?" Deedee asked with concern.

"Need any help?" Tim asked.

"No," I shouted at them, too. "No, I don't need any help." I turned to Tim. "Certainly not from you. And you can have your old candy wrapper back."

"Candy wrapper?" Tim asked.

"Candy wrapper?" Midge said.

"Forget it. All of you forget it," I said, and started eating Midge's rice pudding. Deedee squeezed my shoulder and took Tim back to their table. I kept shoveling in the rice pudding, until the dish was empty. Then I turned to Midge. "I think it was cold beans."

I looked at Cliff, and then at Oliver, and then at Mike, and then I laughed loudly. Oliver started up, too, and suddenly we were all laughing and banging each other on the backs. Tears ran down my face, but they were happy tears. The tension had been broken, at least for the moment. And I had said what I felt. No matter what, I had said what I felt.

153

Chapter Fifteen

When I woke up the morning of the Spring Dance, I stretched in bed and gazed out of my window. It was a perfect day, cloudless and warm with a breeze that rustled the new leaves on the trees and gently shook the screens in the windows. I had pressed my dress, with help from Grandma, the night before and it hung from the top of my closet door, falling gracefully into folds. The morning sun made the lilac color of the gown softer and more delicate, and I knew that at the Inn it would deepen and catch the moving lights.

A half-finished poem was in my typewriter on the desk. I had started it the day before, trying to capture some of the feelings I had about myself and the never-to-be-heard-from-again Romeo. It was harder than almost any other poem I had written, harder to express my feelings about this unknown, nameless boy and what he had meant to me.

I was looking forward to being with Oliver. He was funny and bright and we meshed in almost every way. Except when he kissed me. It was nice and sweet and pleasant, but I knew there should be more. I had never felt the more, but I wasn't going to let that spoil the night.

I got out of bed and ran downstairs to the kitchen. The house was strangely silent. I knew Barb was still sleeping. I looked out of the kitchen window and saw Grandma weeding the herb garden she kept. "Where's Mother?" I called to her.

"She's at the supermarket. She's going out for the day with Walt and wanted to get the shopping done early."

I was getting used to Walt. Not that Mother saw him constantly, but he took her out about once a week, and now I was able to talk to him without feeling my stomach turn over. Actually, he was a nice man. He didn't have my father's humor or vibrancy or zaniness, but Walt was gentle and kind and I knew he understood my mixed feelings about him.

I poured some juice and fixed a bowl of dry cereal for myself. As I sat at the table, I mentally listed all the things I had to do to get ready for the dance. Then I ran upstairs, washed, put on jeans — baggy ones — and a T-shirt. I felt restless and wanted to be with Midge. I stopped on the way out and called to Grandma, "I'm going over to see Midge."

"Okay," she yelled back.

I jogged at a good pace and when I reached the Roth house I ran in, still maintaining my jogging rhythm. "Where are you, Midge?" I called out.

"In the kitchen," she answered.

She was literally up to her elbows in chicken parts and other assorted things. Her mother was seated at the kitchen table, watching her with an unbelieving expression on her face.

"What are you *doing?*" I asked.

"I'm making *poulet avec champignons et carottes*," she answered, never taking her eyes off of the chicken she was dipping in flour.

"Why are you doing that on the day of the dance?" I asked.

Midge now looked up. "I saw this recipe

156

last night in a magazine and had to try it. That's how you build a good catering service. You collect recipes for years and have a solid selection to fall back on."

"How can you want to mess around the kitchen this morning?"

Mrs. Roth said, "I asked her the same thing."

Midge's blue eyes snapped with anger. "Would you find it so odd to write a poem this morning?"

I thought of the half-written poem in my typewriter. "No. I just never thought of cooking in the same way."

Midge looked me right in the eyes, daring me to argue further. "You write; I cook."

I sat down next to Mrs. Roth. "I'm sorry, Midge. Really. I just can't get used to someone cooking for pleasure, I guess. Except Grandma. But you're right. I write and you cook."

Midge glanced at me with her usual warmth again. "I'll be through soon, and then we can talk."

"It's okay. I have to go home anyway and do some things. I'll see you tonight."

Midge waved a floury hand at me as I left.

* * *

In the late afternoon, I began my preparations for the dance. Cleopatra couldn't have taken as much time getting ready for Marc Antony as I did preparing for Oliver. I relaxed in a bubble bath that came up to my chin, closing my eyes and picturing the serenest things I knew — my cousin's farm in Vermont with the gentle hills and cows grazing; the beach at Nantucket Sound when the tide was out and there was barely a ripple in the water; a cat sleeping in the sun. While I imagined all these things, I remembered not to get so relaxed that I drowned. I could see the headlines: POET DIES ON DAY OF SPRING DANCE.

I washed my hair twice and dried it until it shot gold lights and curled around my head. I let the curls fly any way they wanted, not trying to subdue them or make them conform to any shape.

I took out the underwear I was going to wear, and the gold sandals, and a tiny gold purse Mother had lent me. I laid them all out on the bed and looked at them. I was excited about going to the dance, but somehow it didn't feel too out of the ordinary to me. It was the way I felt when I looked at pictures of the Colosseum in Rome. I felt that when I saw it in person, and some day I knew I would, it would seem familiar and

158

right that I should be there. That was the way I felt the day of the dance.

At dinner time, Grandma and Barbara were more uptight than I was, reminding me that I still had to get ready. Barbara said between mouthfuls of lamb stew, "What kind of flowers is Oliver going to give you?"

"I don't know. I mean, I couldn't say bring orchids or some rare tropical flower. So I just told him what color my dress was and I hoped he wouldn't bring something orange."

Barbara raised her eyes to the ceiling. "With Oliver's taste, he'll bring something awful. What's *he* wearing?"

I put down my fork. "You really are a superficial child. What difference does it make? I'm going with Oliver, not his clothes. As it happens, he's borrowing his father's tuxedo, because he doesn't want to spend the money to rent one. And I think he's right. And before you ask, it's *black*."

"Ugh," Barbara said definitely.

Mother and Grandma both said at the same time, "Barbara!"

Mother looked at Grandma. "How did we get that girl? I mean we all have what I like to think of as decent values here. What did we do wrong with her?"

Barbara laughed and went on eating. "Come on, all of you. I'm just as good as Juliet, only a little more surface-oriented." She looked very pleased with herself.

"Surface-oriented," Mother repeated. "Where did you get that from?"

Barbara took the pitcher of water on the table and filled her glass. "That's what Cliff says I am. He says it's just a stage."

We laughed but I admired Barb for being able to accept herself as she was, without feeling she had to be like me or Mother or anyone else. I hoped she'd stay that way, even if it meant being some things that I didn't particularly like.

I went upstairs, and started what was going to be the hardest part for me, putting on makeup. I never wore much and never thought about how it went on. I just put it on. But tonight I wanted the makeup to be a part of me, not dumped on my face. Mother came into the bathroom as I was staring at myself in the mirror. "Want some help with your makeup?"

"I'd love it."

She took my hand and led me into her bathroom, which had a small dressing table in a corner. I sat there and she tilted my face up and delicately put on foundation and powder and some blusher. "It's gilding the lily," she said, "but it looks good."

She added a little eye makeup and pale pink lip gloss. "Take a look."

I turned to the mirror and liked what I saw. I didn't look "made-up" at all. My face just looked smoother and pinker and my eyes darker and bigger. "I like it," I said.

Mother put a finger under my chin and raised my face. "You're very beautiful. You look like your father. What's nice is, you don't even know you're that pretty. Keep it that way, because it doesn't really matter, in the whole scheme of life, whether you're pretty. It doesn't hurt, but it doesn't matter."

She helped me slip my dress on, smoothed it in all the right places, and stepped back. "Deedee's dress is perfect on you."

I opened my closet door and looked in the full-length mirror nailed to the inside. Mother was right. The dress hung softly on me, making me look, as Deedee had said, like Cathy Earnshaw and Diana Ross. From downstairs, Grandma called up. "Oliver is here."

I walked down the stairs slowly to affect a grand entrance, yet I was embarrassed at wanting to. Oliver was in the living room, talking to Barbara. He turned as I came in and simply said, "Wow!" Then he came over to me and handed me a florist's box. "If ever I saw a person who looks like a poet, it's you."

The flowers were small, delicate, purple-and-white blooms made into a wrist corsage. I slipped them on. "They're perfect. Barbara was worried you'd bring something weird."

"*Juliet*," Barbara said with annoyance.

Oliver turned to her. "Me, Barb? The epitome of taste and sophistication?" He hesitated, then laughed. "Anyway, my mother picked them out. I wanted to bring hollyhocks, but she didn't think they would look so good on Juli's wrist."

Oliver had his family car and we drove the few miles to the Dellwood Inn, talking about who would be at the dance. The Inn looked like your garden variety hotel, but it seemed beautiful to me that night. The room the dance was in was big and decorated in red and gold. A small band was playing and a few couples were on the dance floor. The rest of the kids were sitting at tables that ringed the dance floor or getting glasses of bright orange punch from the refreshment table on the side. I tried to think of what could make the drink that color, but then decided it was better not to know.

Midge and Davey were dancing and talking animatedly — *both* of them. Deedee and Tim were sitting at a table with Jim and his date. Deedee saw me and waved wildly. I tried not to look at Tim, sitting next to her, his blond hair catching the moving light.

The room was gaudy and noisy and crowded, but I loved it. I loved dancing the fast numbers, feeling my body take on a life of its own, moving to the music. I loved the slow dances, being held close to whoever the boy of the moment was. I loved laughing with Midge and seeing Davey relax and joke with Oliver and me. I loved drinking the mystery punch and eating silly little cookies and ridiculous little sandwiches. I loved talking to Deedee in the women's room about who was there with whom. The only moments I wasn't happy were when I saw Tim dancing with someone, laughing with someone, carrying glasses of punch to his table. Then I was filled with such monumental yearning that I hardly knew what to do. But it would pass and again I would be wonderfully happy.

And then came the moment I knew
would come, when Tim asked me for our
one dance. He held me lightly in his arms,
as always. I moved closer to him and put
my cheek against his. His arm tightened
around me and we danced in silence. After
a few moments I heard him take a deep
breath and say, so softly I could hardly
hear him:

"It is my lady;
O, it is my love!
O that she knew she were."

I heard the words. I heard the voice, but
there were no connective thoughts for a
moment. Then I focused my eyes on a light
that whirled back and forth across the far
wall, and tried to think. I held on to Timothy more tightly, for he was solidity in a
room that was spinning along with the
lights and the dancers. *Not Timothy. Not
possible.*

He brought me even closer to him and
now in a clearer, firmer voice, said:

"But soft!
What light through yonder window breaks?
It is the East, and Juliet is the sun!"

I moved away so I could look into his
green eyes. "You, Tim? *You* are the one?"

He nodded his head, not speaking.

"Why?" I asked.

He brought me close in his arms again, resting his cheek on my hair. "Because I love you and I couldn't tell you."

Couldn't tell you! Couldn't tell you. The words echoed in my head, making no sense.

"Juli, could we go outside where it's quiet and talk for a few minutes?"

I looked around the room and saw Oliver dancing with Midge, and Deedee dancing with some boy I didn't know. Tim took my hand and we walked out of the room, out of the Dellwood Inn. There was a bench under a tree on the large, perfectly trimmed lawn outside the hotel. We sat down and for a moment neither of us spoke.

Then I said in a voice that surprised me with its strength and firmness, "Tim, I have loved you for years. I would have died for one sign from you that you cared about me. Why didn't you tell me?"

Tim took me by the shoulders and turned me toward him. "You love *me?* You mean that?" His voice was filled with wonderment and anguish, too.

I was Juliet, as ever, realistic Juliet. "How could you be so dense? Why do you sound as if it would be impossible for me to love you? Tim, I don't understand anything you're saying."

He got up and started moving around.

Walking behind the tree, leaving me sitting alone, returning to the bench, then walking around the tree again. Finally, he stopped moving and stood in front of me. "Juli, you're everything wonderful. You're smart, you're a writer, and you're beautiful. Look at your friends. They're all geniuses — Cliff, Oliver. I'm a lightweight by comparison. Why should I have thought you'd love me?"

I stood up and put my hands on either side of his face. "Tim, don't you know you're one of the golden people at school? You're part of that inaccessible world that other kids yearn to be part of. Doesn't that mean anything to you?"

He pulled me down onto the bench and sat next to me, holding my hands so tightly that I felt my bones might snap. "Juliet, there's no one in that 'inaccessible world' that matches you, that comes near you. I know I'm good-looking. I know I'm pleasant, friendly, maybe even what people call charming. But you, you're special. You're unique. There are millions of guys and girls like me all around, but you, Juliet, are *one* in a million."

I felt we had talked enough for the moment. So I leaned over and gently put my lips on his, kissing him softly, hoping the kiss would tell him what I was feeling. He remained still. Then he put his arms around me and pulled me to him, kissing me with an intensity I had never felt before. I returned his kiss with the same fervor, until we broke apart breathlessly. We clung to each other, murmuring, mumbling all the usual phrases that seemed so unused. "I can't believe it." "It's amazing." "I love you." "When did you first — ?" "How long?" "Why?"

Tim held me by the shoulders and looked deep into my eyes. "Why me, Juli?"

I leaned my head on his shoulder. "Don't you know how special *you* are? Kind and dear and caring. You even have nice candy wrappers."

Tim shook me slightly. "We're back with the candy wrappers. What's it mean?"

"Another time," I said. Then reality descended. "Tim, we have to go back. Oliver and Deedee will be looking for us. I can't hurt Oliver."

"I know," Tim agreed. "Deedee will be okay. She's nuts about Henry Winberg."

"How did you know?"

Tim grinned. "Did you ever see the way she looks at him?" He kissed me gently

167

again and we walked back to the Inn. "Can I see you tomorrow afternoon? We have a lot to talk about."

"I'd love it." I brushed my face against his arm. My head was spinning with what had happened, and also with how I was going to cope with this. Then I remembered. "Tim, why the phone calls? They were wonderful, but strange."

Tim almost giggled with embarrassment. "Well, like I said, I couldn't tell you I loved you, because I thought you'd laugh or brush me off or wouldn't give a damn. But I wanted to be close to you in some way, to tell you without your knowing it was me. I had my copy of the play left over from last year's English class, so I just . . . used it."

He put his arms around me again. "I guess I thought you'd like the Romeo bit. I mean, I felt that was the kind of thing that would please you, poetry and all that. And I wanted to do something that was meant just for you."

The rest of the night passed in a dream-like, spectral way. The shadowy parts were what was happening every minute; the crystal-clear parts were the unreality of Tim and I in love. I danced and ate and laughed and every moment I was aware of where Tim was in the room. I never had to look. I just knew. Now he is dancing with Deedee; now he is in the left-hand corner; now he is eating a sandwich; now he isn't here at all. When I did raise my eyes to look for him, he was always watching me. We were separated for the rest of the night, but totally together.

Midge and Davey and Oliver and I went to the Donut Hut after the dance for an early breakfast. My head ached furiously and I could hardly keep my eyes open, but I dutifully ate eggs and drank coffee. Often I caught Midge looking at me curiously, and I'd smile until my lips felt they were going to snap at the corners. Finally, she said, "I'm going to the women's room. Want to come?"

I went along, my feet hardly seeming to touch the floor. When she shut the door she turned to me immediately, *"What's with you?* If I didn't know you better, I'd say you were drunk or stoned."

How could I *not* tell her? She was Midge Roth, my dearest friend in all this unreal world. We had been confidantes since kindergarten. We had laughed, cried, studied, dreamed, and even had chicken pox together. "Tim and I are in love," I said as succinctly as I could. "Please don't ask me any questions tonight. I'll talk to you tomorrow." I drifted out of the room, leaving her staring after me.

When Oliver took me home, he shut off the car engine and turned to me. "The Juliet I brought to the dance is not the same Juliet I am bringing home."

Oliver was too sensitive, too tuned in to people, not to have been aware of *something* happening. He leaned over and kissed my cheek. "I'll talk to you tomorrow." He walked me to the front door, stood with me while I unlocked it, kissed my cheek again, and went back to his car. "I'll talk to you tomorrow," he said again.

I'm going to have an awful lot of people to talk to tomorrow, I thought.

I was grateful that no one in the house was awake. I couldn't talk to another person. Mother's door was open and I gently, silently closed it. It was a signal we had. She left her door open when she went to sleep. When I got home at night I closed her door. Then if she woke up during the night, she knew by a quick look whether I was home or not.

I went into my bedroom and sank to the

floor, not turning on the lights. I rested my head against the windowsill and watched the sky lighten. There was a lot to think about, but I couldn't think about anything, not even Tim's loving me. I fell asleep with my head on the sill, woke up an hour later, took off my clothes, and stumbled into bed.

Chapter Sixteen

It seemed like a lifetime ago, that morning Mother woke me to tell me Mike was on the phone. Now she was standing by my bed again. This time she had the phone with her, and she handed it to me. "It's Timothy Thornton." She raised her eyebrows and went out, closing the door behind her.

"Hi," I said almost shyly.

"She speaks. O, speak again, bright angel!" Tim whispered into the phone.

I laughed and stretched every muscle in my body. "Have you memorized *all* of *Romeo and Juliet*?"

"I could lie, try to impress you, and say yes, but, no, I haven't, but I do have a very dog-eared copy of the play." He paused. "I love you, Juliet. I don't need Will Shakespeare to say *that* for me now."

"I love you, too, Tim," I answered.

"Listen, how would you like to go for a drive this afternoon? Maybe to that new museum in New Haven? It's eleven o'clock. I could pick you up at twelve-thirty, and we'll have some lunch along the way."

"I'd like that," I said. "I've been wanting to see the museum."

"I thought you would," he said. "See you at twelve-thirty."

I hung up the phone and lay quietly in bed. I knew Tim was going to the New Haven Museum because he thought I'd want to. That was like Tim, and he wondered why I loved him. Now that I was awake, my head was filled with questions again. Should I tell the people who knew about Romeo that it was Tim? What should I say to Oliver and Mike and Cliff? What should I say to Deedee? How do you suddenly appear with a new boyfriend like Timothy Thornton?

Mother knocked on the door, came in, and took the phone out of my hands. She put it back on the table in the hall and sat down on my bed. "Want to give your old mother a small hint of what is going on?"

I smiled. "Well, a small one. I'm going out with Tim this afternoon. In fact, in an hour and a half." That was all I wanted to say now, until I could talk to Tim some more.

"Well," she said, "you did what I asked — that certainly was a *small* hint. Take a shower, get dressed, and I'll fix you some breakfast." She turned away and then back again. "I almost forgot in the excitement of the dream boy calling — how was the dance?"

"Wonderful," I said, sighing. "Wonderful!"

"It seems so!" She smiled and walked out of the room.

When Tim picked me up, he seemed totally relaxed and at ease with my family. He charmed Grandma just by being Tim. He engaged Mother by being really interested in her work, and he entranced Barb just by breathing. Tim was naturally at ease with people; naturally interested in them; naturally a nice man.

When we were in the car, I turned to him. "Tim, I do want to go to the museum some time, and I love you for suggesting it, but today could we just pick up some food and picnic and talk and, well, get to know each other better?"

"Sure!" Tim answered. "Museums are not *really* my first choice for a Sunday afternoon. But don't worry," he added hurriedly, "I'll learn!"

We stopped at a small grocery store and bought sandwich makings, and soft drinks, and fruit, and cookies, and rode out to Dellwood Park. Everything in Dellwood was named Dellwood something or other — old John Dell made sure of that. The park was warm and green; the air was soft and sweet. We sat near the lake. Tim had taken an old raincoat from the trunk of the car and spread the food out on it. Then he leaned over and kissed me. It was the softest kiss, and the sweetest, I had ever had. Not that I'd had that many. He put his head in my lap and looked up at me. Shadows from the swaying leaves moved on his face and his eyes were as green as the new grass we were sitting on.

"I don't believe any of this," he said. "I don't believe that Juliet Gibson, poet, loves me."

"How did you know? About the poet bit, I mean?"

"Word gets around when there is a celebrity in Dellwood."

I felt tense suddenly. "You're not joking about my writing poetry? I take it very seriously."

Tim sat up and took my face in his hands. "Juliet, don't! I may not be a great intellectual myself, but I take everything about you seriously, even the things I don't understand. You and I are different, I know, but that's part of what I love about you."

"I'm sorry, Tim," I said. "I didn't mean to hurt you." Then I said, "Tim, a lot of people know about Romeo's calls. Well, Mother, Grandma, Midge, and Barbara, anyway. What do I say to them? Everyone is still trying to figure out who the caller was. What should I do?"

Tim was thoughtful for a few minutes. "Damn, Juli, I don't want the whole world knowing what should be private between you and me. It would be pretty embarrassing for me to come to your house, knowing your whole family is aware I made the calls. I'd hate it!"

I sighed. "I understand. You're right. I won't say anything, and I know their interest will die out eventually. Please don't worry."

He put his arms around me and kissed my nose. "Good."

I huddled in his arms and said, more plaintively than I wanted to, "Midge? How can I not tell Midge? My best friend."

Tim threw back his head and laughed that wonderful Tim laugh. "Okay, Midge. She's a good kid." He stopped. "She won't tell anyone else? Can you trust her?"

"With my life," I answered dramatically.

"Only it's not your life, it's *mine*," Tim said equally dramatically.

He opened the bread and packages of meat and started making sandwiches, while I spread out the fruit and cookies and paper plates we had brought. "Then there's Oliver and Mike and Cliff. We've been friends for so long. You're not one of those unreasonable, jealous types, are you? Those boys are important to me, and I'm going to go on being friends with them."

Tim sat back on his heels. "Juliet. Of course I'm a jealous type. Most people in love are jealous to a reasonable, sane degree. But your friends are your friends. Deedee is my friend and I'm going to keep her as a friend, too."

"Do you think she'll be upset about us?" I asked.

"I told her on the way home last night,"

he confessed. "She said to tell you now she can go all out after Henry. Poor Henry doesn't have a chance."

The rest of the afternoon we talked. About things that happened when we were kids, about how we felt about our parents, about school, and about how much we loved each other and why. We kissed and ate and lay back on the grass on our backs and watched the sun move across the sky. We threw a Frisbee around that Tim found in the car. And we agreed that I was much better at it than he was. The Frisbee Queen, he called me. By the time he drove me home, we were beginning to know each other. He knew I hated mustard; I knew he loathed fish. He knew I was afraid of moths; I knew he was afraid of snakes. He knew I was great at Frisbee and terrible at tennis; I knew he was a great swimmer and awful at basketball. He knew I loved him; I knew he loved me. He knew I was against nuclear armament; I knew he was against the draft. He knew I was still missing my father dreadfully; I knew he felt uncomfortable with his. We were reaching out to each other.

When he finally took me home, we sat in his car for a few minutes and he held me against him, kissing the side of my face every now and then. "I'll pick you up in the morning, and we'll go to school together. That will announce to the world that Juliet Gibson and Timothy Thornton are a couple to end all couples."

I was nervous. I couldn't help imagining Mike's face and Oliver's and Cliff's when they saw me with Tim. But there was no point in not facing reality. "Okay," I said.

I had called Midge after I had spoken to Tim that morning and asked her to come over for dinner. When I walked into my house I heard her in the kitchen, talking to Grandma. "Midge?" I called out. "Come on upstairs while I change my clothes."

As soon as we got up to my room, I shut the door, and poured out the whole story of the night before and the wonderful afternoon I'd had.

"I'd be totally happy, if it weren't for the boys. I don't want to hurt them. What are they going to say and feel when they know about Tim?"

"They don't own you," Midge said with vehemence. "Anyway, I think what you said that day in the cafeteria is true. The competition with each other is more important than you are. That sounds awful. I don't mean that they don't like you, but

179

it would kill each one of them if you picked *one* of *them* over the other two."

"I hope you're right."

Midge stretched out on my bed and raised her hands over her head. "I'll bet it won't bother them as much as you think, since you're choosing Tim and not one of them. Anyway, you're your own person. You have a perfect right to go out with whomever you want, and the sooner those guys know it the better."

I started to put a clean T-shirt on and mumbled while I was pulling it over my head, "And what about Deedee? I like her."

"Honestly, Juli," Midge said firmly, "you're just looking for trouble. Tim told you Deedee didn't mind. And you know she likes Henry, so what's the big deal you're making?"

But later that night, after Midge had gone, I pulled the phone into my room and called Deedee. She responded with immediate warmth. "Hey, Tim told me last night you and he are going together. I think it's great. He's a good guy. Almost good enough for you."

I breathed easier. "You sure you don't mind?"

"Juli, Tim was never a real romance to me. Now Henry — that's another thing."

I twisted the phone cord nervously. "Well, *you* may not mind but everyone in school is going to think I'm a rotten girl who steals other people's boyfriends. I'll hate that."

Deedee was silent. Then she said, "Go to sleep. Don't worry, and I'll take care of everything."

"How?" I asked plaintively.

Deedee laughed softly. "You'll see tomorrow. Go to sleep."

And I did.

The next morning, Tim was at the house when I finished breakfast. The number of looks Mother and Grandma and Barbara exchanged were beyond counting, but I tried to ignore them. "Have some orange juice," Grandma said when the silence became thick. Tim smiled and took a glass from Grandma, drinking it quickly.

"Come on, Juliet, we'll be late," he said after he put the glass down.

I blew a kiss to Mother and Grandma, made a face at Barb, who was staring at Tim unashamedly, and went out with Tim. When we got out of the house, he leaned over and kissed me quickly. "Good morning."

We walked to school briskly. When we

reached the high school, he took my hand firmly in his as we walked up the steps to the doors. At the top of the steps Deedee stood smiling. "You were afraid the world was going to think you were a rotten person, so I'm here to keep your reputation unsullied."

She walked next to me with her arm around my shoulders. I felt like a lamb going to the slaughter with Tim holding my hand and Deedee's arm around me. Almost everyone that passed us did a double take. Deedee just kept smiling and talking to me nonstop. "See. Now everyone will know you and Tim have my blessings."

When we got to her first class, she squeezed my hand, waved at Tim, and went into the room. I leaned against the wall, exhausted. Tim pulled me away and walked me to my classroom. At the door he said, "Of course, you know lunch time is going to be the real test. We'll have to take on the cafeteria."

I thought of the three boys sitting at our table and closed my eyes for a second. From a distance I heard Tim. "Where is your last class before lunch? I'll meet you there."

I came back to life suddenly. "No, don't,

Tim. Give me a little time alone with the boys. Okay?"

"Sure, you're right. I'll see you sometime during lunch." He squeezed my shoulder affectionately and walked away.

All through the morning I kept thinking what I would say to Mike, to Oliver, to Cliff. I rehearsed dozens of brilliant, ridiculous, meaningless statements and discarded all of them. I couldn't believe this was happening. Here I was with what I had always wanted — Tim caring about me — and all I could do was worry about the three boys. Life made no sense to me at all.

As soon as I walked into the cafeteria at lunch time, I saw them at our table. Midge and Davey Feiner were there, too. I didn't know if that was going to make things any better, but it couldn't make them any worse. I sat down at the table and said too loudly and cheerfully, "Hi, everybody."

They all looked at me silently. Finally Oliver said, "Hi?"

I rearranged my books on the table about five times and then plunged in. "Look, I want to tell you guys something." I stopped.

"So?" Mike said. "What is it?"

I cleared my throat. "Well, it's like this. I'm going to be dating Tim Thornton from now on. Uh, quite a lot, I think. I just wanted to tell you, so that ... so that you'd know."

Oliver was the first one to say anything. "*That's* what happened Saturday night. That's why I felt you were different when I took you home. Right?"

I nodded my head. Mike and Cliff were still perfectly silent, staring at me accusingly.

"Look," I said firmly. "None of you really, well, really *love* me. We're friends. We'll always be friends; Tim won't change that. But we've never been romantic about each other. Be honest. You may have *thought* you felt that way, but you didn't really. You know it."

The table was silent again. Midge desperately started joking, "A funny thing happened on the way to school today ..." No one even looked at her. "Well," she said feebly, "maybe it wasn't *that* funny."

Finally Mike asked, "Why Tim? I mean why Tim and not me or Cliff or Oliver?"

I shrugged miserably. "I don't know. I can't explain it, really. Why is one person so attractive to you and not another? I

184

guess it's partly chemical or magical or who knows what. It just seems to be. I can't give you any sensible answers."

The boys looked at me silently. I felt I had to say something more. And I realized something important. I spoke quickly, gathering assurance as I went on.

"Partly, it's because, each one of you likes one aspect of me and is mainly interested in just that. You, Oliver, like me because I like poetry and writing. You, Mike, like me because I like sports. You, Cliff, like me because I like to think about life and people. But not one of you sees me as a whole, total person. Tim doesn't like me because I bowl or write or have deep dreams. He just likes Juliet Gibson."

The boys looked at me thoughtfully. Now I knew I was right. "Oliver, what would you have done if I had told you I wasn't interested in writing anymore or reading the books you like? You wouldn't have hung around long. And you, Mike, if I told you I didn't want to bowl or bike-ride or come to the games, you wouldn't be much interested in me. And the same goes for you, Cliff. I don't have to excel at anything, unless *I* want to, for Tim to care about me. I like that."

Finally, Mike said, "Well, he's a pretty

nice guy. Lousy basketball player, but he's a nice guy."

Oliver agreed. "Yeah, can't write worth a damn, but he's okay."

And then Cliff joined in. "Probably doesn't know anything about dream symbols, but I guess he's okay, too."

I saw Tim hovering in the back of the cafeteria, watching us, and I waved to him to come over. When he reached the table, there was a lot of moving of chairs to make room for him, mumbled greetings, back-slapping, and general uneasiness. When Tim finally squeezed into a small space, we all sat in silence. Then Mike said to Tim, "Uh, a gang of us are going bowling Friday night. Want to come? With Juliet."

Tim grinned. "Sure." He turned to me. "Okay with you?"

"Sure. Fine." I flashed Mike a grateful smile.

Then everyone was talking at once. Tim said to me, "Want to get something to eat?"

I stood up and we walked to the back of the cafeteria, got trays, and moved along the line, looking at the food. When we reached the desserts I stopped and gazed at the chocolate cake. "I love it."

Tim smiled. "It's my absolute favorite."

We stood perfectly still, gazing at each

other happily. Then in front of the whole cafeteria Tim leaned over and kissed my cheek. From the back of the line a boy yelled out, "Hey, Romeo, move it! You're holding up the whole works."

Tim threw back his head and laughed and I leaned against the rail, laughing just as hard. Then Tim reached over and put a slice of chocolate cake on my tray. "Juliet, dear fair one," he said dramatically, "my first gift to you."